The Caribbean Cruise Caper

Joe lay on his bunk in the darkness, listening intently. Something had disturbed him. What?

After a few moments he heard furtive scraping sounds. His mental map told him they were coming from the corridor just outside the door to his cabin.

Stealthily Joe pushed back the covers and stood up. He tiptoed across the dark cabin, felt his way along the wall to the door, and opened it a crack. The light in the corridor, which was left on all the time, was off. A bad sign—someone must have unscrewed a bulb.

A faint, almost indetectable glimmer of light came from the main deck. Joe walked silently along the corridor toward it.

Suddenly a shape loomed up in front of him, cutting off the light. He sensed, more than saw, two hands reaching out to grab him.

The Hardy Boys Mystery Stories

Available from MINSTREL Books

THE HARDY BOYS®

154

THE CARIBBEAN CRUISE CAPER

FRANKLIN W. DIXON

A MINSTREL® BOOK

Published by POCKET BOOKS

New York London Toronto Sydney Tokyo Singapore

This book is a work of fiction. Names, characters, places and incidents are products of the author's imagination or are used fictitiously. Any resemblance to actual events or locales or persons, living or dead, is entirely coincidental.

A MINSTREL PAPERBACK *Original*

A Minstrel Book published by
POCKET BOOKS, a division of Simon & Schuster Inc.
1230 Avenue of the Americas, New York, NY 10020

Copyright © 1999 by Simon & Schuster Inc.

Front cover illustration by John Youssi

ISBN: 0-671-02549-X

First Minstrel Books printing January 1999

10 9 8 7 6 5 4 3 2 1

THE HARDY BOYS MYSTERY STORIES is a trademark of Simon & Schuster Inc.

THE HARDY BOYS, A MINSTREL BOOK and colophon are registered trademarks of Simon & Schuster Inc.

Printed in the U.S.A.

Contents

THE CARIBBEAN
CRUISE CAPER

1 Flight to the Islands

Eighteen-year-old Frank Hardy slowly turned his head to the left, then to the right. He shrugged his shoulders forward and back, then winced. The flight south from New York to the Caribbean had left him with a major crick in his neck. Airline seats were not very friendly to six-footers like him and his younger brother, Joe.

Joe, seventeen, scanned the crowd of eager vacationers in the San Juan, Puerto Rico, airport. He brushed his blond hair back from his forehead. "Can you spot David anywhere?" he asked.

Frank shook his head. A little jab of pain at the base of the skull made him wish he hadn't.

"Nope," he replied. "Don't worry, though. He'll turn up. He didn't bring us all this way just to strand us."

1

David Wildman, their host, was a playwright. His suspense thriller, *Stairway to Oblivion,* had been an off-Broadway hit. He was now running *Teenway* magazine's teen-detective contest. The five teenage finalists were to spend a week on a luxurious yacht in the Caribbean. There they would compete in solving a series of staged mysteries. The grand prize was a college scholarship.

David had asked Frank and Joe to come along as expert consultants. He knew about their skill and growing fame as detectives from a fellow playwright they had helped.

"This won't be nearly as exciting as tackling real crimes," he had explained apologetically. "These are more like complicated puzzles. But your presence, your experience, will be enormously helpful. You'll love the yacht, the *Colombe d'Or,* and the islands are beautiful this time of year."

The Hardys had agreed. Now here they were in Puerto Rico, and the *Colombe d'Or* was waiting for them and the other passengers a few islands away.

Frank glanced at his watch, then studied the Arrivals column on the overhead TV monitor. "David and the others should be here by now," he remarked. "The flight from Miami landed a few minutes ago."

"Joe, Frank," someone called. "Over here!"

Frank looked around. David was easy to pick out from the crowd of brightly clad tourists. He was wearing his usual outfit of black jeans, black T-shirt, and thick-soled black workboots. His sandy hair, receding at the temples, was pulled back into a little ponytail. He had a leather case for a laptop computer slung over one shoulder.

The Hardys threaded their way over to him. He put his hands on their shoulders and turned to the little group around him. "Gang, meet Joe and Frank Hardy, superdetectives," he said. "I'm hoping they'll tell us about some of their cases later."

Frank had looked over the list of contestants during the flight down. As David introduced them, he tried to pin mental tags on them. He would get to know them better pretty quickly.

Elizabeth Wheelwright was a tall, slim, blond preppie from Virginia. She was standing a small but noticeable distance apart from the others. She gave Frank and Joe a cool nod. She seemed to take it for granted that David would introduce her first.

Cesar Ariosto, standing next to her, noticed this and gave her a mocking grin. He was about five nine, with long black hair and the shadow of a mustache on his upper lip. He wore a silver-and-turquoise bracelet on his left wrist and had a bad case of nail biting.

"Cesar's from Albuquerque," David said. "And this is Jason MacFarlane, from Fort Worth."

"Yo, what's happening, dudes?" Jason said. He was wearing baggy jeans and a sleeveless T-shirt with the picture of a hot heavy-metal group. His dark hair was cut very short on top and long in back.

A boy of about ten in shorts and a long green

soccer shirt tugged at David's elbow. "Hey, what about me?" he demanded.

David smiled. "This is my son, Evan. Evan is currently in the doghouse," he added, with a pretend scowl.

"Oh? Why?" Joe asked.

"A little matter of some black plastic bugs," David replied. "On the flight down, they somehow found their way into our salads. The flight attendants were not amused."

"They were so," Evan said. "They laughed like anything when you couldn't see them."

"Evan—no more practical jokes. Is that clear?" David said.

Evan nodded. His expression made Frank wonder if his fingers were crossed behind his back.

"And these are our remaining finalists, Sylvie de Carabas and Boris Lebidof," David continued. "Sylvie is from near Montreal. Boris was born in Russia and now lives in Brooklyn."

"'Allo," Sylvie said, with a charming accent. Her blue eyes twinkled at them. "We will have much fun, no?"

Boris nodded to them. He had a narrow face topped by unruly blond hair. From the look of his shoulders and upper arms, Frank guessed that working out was a major hobby of his.

"Hold it," someone called. A light flashed. When the spots cleared from Frank's eyes, he saw a guy of about seventeen with straight black hair and almond eyes. He had two fancy cameras slung around his neck. He was wearing jeans and a khaki photographer's vest over a Day-Glo orange *Teenway* T-shirt.

"Meet Kenneth Lee," David said. "He'll be part of our band, too. He and Lisa are working as interns at the mag."

"Hi, Kenneth," Frank said. He looked over at Kenneth's companion. Lisa was also about seventeen, with pixie-cut light brown hair. Her brown eyes were partly hidden behind thick black-framed glasses. In one hand she held a slender black microcassette recorder.

"Lisa Burnham," she said. "I'll be covering this event for the magazine. Tell me, Joe, Frank—you guys have tackled real crimes. How does it feel to be part of the *Teenway* teen detective contest?"

She pointed the recorder at Joe.

"Great!" Joe said, grinning.

When the recorder was swung around to Frank, he said, "Joe's our spokesperson."

"Come on, guys, loosen up," Lisa said. "You can do better than that."

"You'll have plenty of time to interview them later, Lisa," David told her. "Right now we have a plane to catch. Anyone see the sign for our gate?"

The group started down a corridor. David explained, "For this last leg, we're on a real puddle jumper," David told Frank and Joe. "We'll take it as far as St. Hilda, where we rendezvous with the *Colombe d'Or.*"

"The column door?" Jason asked. "That's a dumb name for a boat."

Sylvie giggled. "Don't be so silly," she said. "It is French. It means 'pigeon of gold.'"

"'Golden dove,'" Elizabeth remarked, just loud enough to be heard.

Sylvie gave her a sidelong look but didn't say anything.

Jason moved up next to Sylvie. "Will you teach me some French?" he asked. "It's such a beautiful language."

Elizabeth rolled her eyes. Frank grinned at Joe. This was starting to look like an interesting bunch.

The airplane was a small two-engine turboprop that seated about twenty passengers. Frank and Joe followed the others up the steps and down the narrow aisle to the rear half of the cabin. Frank grabbed a seat across from Lisa.

"So . . . how long have you worked at *Teenway?*" he asked her.

"Oh, I don't really work for the magazine," she replied, coloring. "I'm just there on a two-month internship. The lowest of the low." She laughed nervously.

"But you said you're covering the teen-detective contest," Frank reminded her. "That's a pretty important assignment, isn't it?"

"It's a terrific opportunity," Lisa said. "But there's no guarantee they'll print my article. One of their staff writers could whip something up out of my information."

The plane taxied to the foot of the runway, and Frank gave up trying to talk over the noise.

He enjoyed takeoffs, partly because of the thrill he got from the element of danger. The pilot released the brakes. The engines roared, pressing him back into his seat. Then the ground dropped away.

The plane banked steeply to the left, out over the water. Frank was looking almost straight down. The parallel lines of surf and the V-shaped wakes of powerboats seemed to spell mysterious messages on the blue sea. The plane leveled off before he could decode them.

It seemed only minutes later that the island of St. Hilda came into sight. It looked like three steep, wooded hills edged by cliffs and a narrow beach with a huddle of buildings clustered around a small bay. Nowhere could Frank spot a patch of level ground large enough for a plane to land.

David, in the seat behind him, leaned forward. "This island is a big hit with people who design flight simulator games," he remarked. "Players go nuts learning how to land here."

"How about our pilot?" Frank asked.

David laughed. "He must have been nuts in the first place even to take the job! The nice thing is, the difficulty of flying in has kept the place unspoiled. There's no way to bring in anything much bigger than this. Oops, hold on. White-knuckle time!"

As the plane banked, Frank saw a short, narrow landing strip cupped by a curving hillside and bordered by the sea. The pilot coasted over the near hilltop and abruptly put the plane into a steep descent. Across the aisle, Lisa gasped loudly.

An instant later the wheels touched down. The propellers screamed in reverse pitch, bringing the plane to a quick stop. The passengers in the front of the cabin started to clap.

"If I were the pilot," David said, "I'd pass the hat after every landing here. I bet I'd make out like a bandit!"

The plane taxied to the terminal, a small building with white stucco walls and a red-tiled roof. The group climbed off the plane and walked across the landing strip.

Frank noticed an outdoor café on one side of the building. A slanted roof of palm fronds shaded the tables from the tropical sun. He nudged Joe. "I don't think we're in Bayport anymore," he murmured.

Joe grinned and put on his sunglasses.

Inside, the terminal was one big, airy room. Near the entrance, in a roped-off area, an official checked the travel documents of the arriving passengers. After David explained to the man who the group was, he waved them through.

A young woman came over. Her polo shirt was embroidered with a palm tree and sun. "We're unloading your luggage now," she told David. "We'll bring it straight to your van."

"Thanks," David said. "We may as well wait outside, then."

He led the group out to the curb. Just then two

8

shiny taxis pulled up with suitcases strapped to their roof racks. While half a dozen passengers got out and started inside the terminal, the drivers lifted down the baggage and stacked it on a nearby wheeled cart. A uniformed porter whistled as he waited next to the cart.

A man with thinning gray hair and a bright Hawaiian print shirt met David's eye. "Hi there," he said. "Just arrive?"

"Right," David replied. "Good stay?"

"Fantastic," the man said. "We hate to leave. You kids will have the time of your life!"

His wife was juggling two straw baskets and a big yellow gourd. "Come on, Charles," she said. "We don't want to miss our plane."

He smiled. "That's not going to happen, Nora. I bet we're the only group flying out right now."

With a nod and a wave, the couple went inside.

A dusty white van turned into the drive and stopped. The driver leaned out to ask, "You are for the yacht club?"

"That's us," David said. He started to bend down, then frowned and looked around sharply.

"Hey!" he exclaimed. "Where's my laptop? It's not here!"

2 A Warm Welcome Aboard

Joe quickly scanned the sidewalk from the curb to the wall of the terminal. He saw nothing that looked like a laptop case.

"What was it in?" he asked David.

"A black leather attaché," David replied. "This isn't funny. All the information about the contest is on my hard drive."

"Maybe you left it on the plane," Boris suggested.

"I'm sure I didn't," David said. "I had it on my shoulder when we came out here. Then I set it down."

He looked around. "Evan?" he continued. "Do you know anything about this?"

The boy looked scared. "No, Daddy, uh-uh," he said. "Not a thing. Really."

"No one in our group has wandered away since we came out here," Frank pointed out. "And no one who *isn't* in our group has come close enough to us to steal something."

"Frank, are you saying this is an impossible crime?" Lisa asked, pointing her recorder at him.

"There's no such thing," Frank retorted. "If it's really impossible, it can't happen."

"I read a story once . . ." Boris began.

"Whoop-de-do," Jason muttered.

Boris ignored him. "This thief had a suitcase with a trick bottom. All he had to do was set the suitcase down on top of whatever he wanted to steal, and *whoosh!* the object vanished."

"I've heard of that gimmick, too," Joe told him. "It sounds pretty clever. But as Frank said, no one came over here with a suitcase. And as for us, we don't even have our suitcases yet. It's probably just some mix-up."

"Here comes our luggage now," Elizabeth said. "It's about time. The workers must all think they're on vacation or something."

"You guys don't seem to understand," David said tensely. "If I've lost all the files on my laptop, that's it for the contest. *Finito!* Kaput!"

Everyone crowded around him and started protesting. Lisa thrust her recorder into the center of the group. Kenneth circled around them, taking one shot after another.

Joe glanced at Frank. "We'd better do something, quick," he said.

"Yeah . . . like find that attaché case," Frank replied. "It couldn't have just walked away."

Joe glanced at the approaching luggage cart. His jaw dropped. "No," he said tautly. "But it might have *rolled* away. I'll be right back."

Joe sprinted into the terminal and across to the runway side. A little cluster of departing passengers was walking across the concrete apron toward the plane. The cart with their baggage was sitting next to the open cargo hatch.

Joe started through the door. A police officer in a light blue uniform, white helmet, and white gunbelt blocked the way. His name tag read L. Mallet.

"Excuse me, sir," he said in a soft, Caribbean-accented voice. "Are you cleared to board this aircraft?"

"No, officer. I just came in on it a few minutes ago," Joe replied. "But I think my friend's computer case got put on that cart by mistake. Do you think you could check for me, please? His name is David Wildman."

Mallet glanced over his shoulder at the plane. Then he said, "Please wait here, sir."

He went over and spoke to the luggage handler. Together they checked the tags on the twenty or so suitcases. Mallet picked up a black leather case and showed it to the group of passengers. They all shook their heads. He returned to Joe, carrying the case.

"Your friend will have to identify this as his property, sir," Mallet said.

"Believe me, he'll be happy to," Joe promised. "I'll go get him."

Joe hurried out and came back with David. After showing Mallet his passport, David unzipped the attaché case to check the contents.

"It doesn't look as if anything's been disturbed," he told Joe. As they started across the waiting room, he added, "What a weird thing. I guess the porter saw my case and thought it belonged to those people who were leaving."

"It could be," Joe said doubtfully. "The way I remember it, though, the porter didn't load the cart. He just stood by. It was the drivers who carried the suitcases from their taxis to the cart. I guess one of them must have picked up your case by mistake."

"Well, however it happened," David said, "I owe you one. If it hadn't been for your quick thinking, my computer and all the contest plans would be on their way back to San Juan by now. I'm tempted to complain to the airport authorities. But we don't know who's responsible. Maybe it's better to let it go."

The moment they returned to the group, the others crowded around. "Oh, good," Elizabeth said. "You found it. An airline lost my bag once in London. I was devastated. I had nothing to wear for four entire days."

"What happened?" Cesar asked Joe. "Where was it?"

Joe laughed. "About to be loaded for a return flight to San Juan."

"So you won't have to call off the contest?" Jason said. "Cool. Let's get going."

"Wait a minute," Boris said. "This is a serious matter. Somebody's dirty trick almost ruined everything for us. We must discover who stole David's computer."

That did it. Five minutes later Joe was seething with frustration. Everyone in the group was a wannabe detective. Each one had his or her far-fetched theory about what had happened, who had done it, and why.

Boris was the worst. After explaining that one of the departing passengers must be in the pay of *Teenway*'s competition, he repeatedly demanded, "It is possible, isn't it? Isn't it?"

Finally Frank told him, "Anything is *possible*, but it just isn't very likely."

For a moment Joe had the feeling that Boris was about to throw a punch at Frank, but then thought better of it. A good thing for him, thought Joe. Boris might have spent a lot of time in the weight room, but Joe could tell by the way he moved that he didn't have Frank's martial arts skills. If attacked, Frank would have decked him.

"We're running late," David said after glancing at his wrist. "We'd better put this off until later. Personally, I think one of the taxi drivers probably made a mistake. But if any of you was responsible for this stunt, I hope you'll have the guts to admit it to me privately. It won't affect your chances in the contest if you do. That's a promise. If *I* find

14

out that one of you did it, that'll be another matter."

Joe met Frank's eyes and saw that he was thinking the same thing. David's threat was pretty empty. Unless one of the group suddenly recalled some crucial fact, the guilty party—if there was one—was not likely to be unmasked.

Everyone crowded into the dusty van for the short ride to the yacht club. The clubhouse was a white wooden building with a shady veranda around all four sides. White wicker tables and chairs were scattered across the lush green lawn.

The yacht club faced a sparkling blue bay, crowded with luxurious boats. As he climbed out of the van, Joe fell in love with a sleek fifty-foot sloop. It looked ready to sail around the world. He decided to sign on as a deckhand . . . once he had talked his dad into giving him permission.

Frank nudged him. "Ground control to Major Joe," he said. "Come in, please."

Joe indicated the sloop. "What do you say we swap *Sleuth* for something along those lines?" *Sleuth* was the name of the Hardys' little outboard runabout.

"Great idea," Frank said with a grin. "We could probably swing it if we threw in three or four hundred thousand bucks on the side."

Cesar joined them. "Can you believe this place?" he said. "There must be millions and millions of dollars' worth of boats out there . . . and this is just one island. Talk about loaded!"

"Successful people are always the targets of envy and jealousy," Elizabeth remarked from a few feet away. She did not look at anyone as she said it, but Joe saw the color rise in Cesar's cheeks. Cesar pressed his lips together as if holding back a retort.

A taxi pulled up next to the van. The woman who got out looked as if she had stepped out of the pages of a fashion magazine's resort issue. She went over to David and pushed her designer sunglasses up on her forehead.

"I was so *determined* to be here to greet you," she said. "Am I hopelessly late? Have you been waiting for me forever?"

David shook his head. "We just arrived," he said. "Gang, I'd like you to meet our hostess on this voyage, the editor of *Teenway*, Bettina Dunn."

He went around the circle, introducing everyone. Bettina had been very well briefed. She seemed to recognize each person and know a little something personal about him or her.

When David came to Joe and said his name, Bettina smiled. "Ah yes—one of the celebrated Hardy brothers. I've met your father. I can see the resemblance. He must be very proud of you. And, of course, this is your brother and partner, Frank."

Joe could not help feeling a warm glow.

When the introductions were finished, Bettina said, "We'll have a more formal welcome after we board the *Colombe d'Or*. For now, I'll just say how pleased all of us at *Teenway* are that you could take part in this thrilling and challenging—and reward-ing—contest."

Everybody clapped.

One of the staff started piling the group's luggage on a wheelbarrow. David kept a tight grip on his computer case.

Bettina led the way into the yacht club. Just inside the door, Joe noticed her stop to say hello to a white-haired man in white slacks and a blue blazer. The man turned away, pretending not to hear her. Bettina reddened and kept walking.

David was a couple of steps ahead. Joe caught up to him. In a low voice, he asked, "You see the elderly man in the blazer? Do you know who he is?"

David raised an eyebrow. "You caught that little exchange, did you? That is Walter Mares. He founded *Teenway*. A few years ago he was forced into retirement after a corporate takeover."

"And Bettina?" Joe asked. "What was her part in the story?"

"She was his discovery," David explained. "His crown princess, I guess you'd say. But when he was kicked out, she stayed on and rose to the top. He took it pretty hard. I doubt if they've spoken to each other since. I hear he's retired now and living down here full-time."

"Are you going to put them in one of your plays?" Joe asked as they stepped onto the veranda and Frank joined them.

David laughed. "I wish I could!"

Frank gave Joe a questioning look. "I'll fill you in later," Joe said.

Evan came running up. "Daddy? Which one is our boat?"

Good question, thought Joe. At least three dozen big motor cruisers and ocean sailers were berthed in the yacht club marina, gleaming in the tropical sunlight.

"That one, son," David said. He pointed toward the end of the finger pier. "The one with the blue smokestack. That's the *Colombe d'Or.*"

Joe's eyes widened. The yacht David indicated dwarfed all the others in the harbor. It was easily half the length of a football field, with two full decks above the water line.

Frank gave a soft whistle.

"Quite an impressive barge, isn't she," David said with a grin. "Some Greek shipping tycoon had her built back in the fifties for his French girlfriend. Then they broke up. After lots of ups and downs, the *Colombe* ended up here in the Caribbean as a charter craft."

Some of the others stopped to listen to David. When he finished, Sylvie said, "I have heard something else about this boat. I have heard that it is under a curse. Terrible things happen to people who sail on it."

3 Along Came a Spider

Sylvie's startling statement was followed by a moment of silence. Then several people spoke at once.

"A curse?" Jason said. "Cool! Are there ghosts, too?"

"What nonsense!" Elizabeth said. Frank thought she sounded a little uneasy.

"Where did you hear this, Sylvie?" asked David.

"It is true, isn't it?" she demanded. "The Greek millionaire who built it disappeared overboard one night. His body was never found. Others, too, have died mysterious deaths."

David raised both hands like a symphony conductor. "Now hold on," he said. "It's true that the boat's first owner vanished at sea. He'd been having some serious money problems. A lot of people thought he must have jumped overboard."

19

"What about the other deaths?" Lisa asked. Frank saw that she was holding her tape recorder at waist level, where it wasn't so obvious.

David rolled his eyes. "People don't always die in hospitals," he said. "Sometimes they die in houses or apartments or hotels or airplanes . . . or aboard yachts. That doesn't mean there's anything sinister or mysterious about their deaths. Sylvie, where did you get all this curse nonsense?"

Sylvie looked away. "There was a magazine article," she muttered.

"Huh!" David exclaimed. "If it's the same one I'm thinking of, it appeared about four years ago, in a supermarket tabloid. How did you stumble across it?"

Frank had to listen hard to hear her reply. "It came by mail last week. A photocopy. There was no name or message."

"Did you notice the postmark?" Frank asked.

Sylvie shook her head. "No, but I'm pretty sure the stamps were U.S., not Canadian."

"Anybody else get a copy of this article?" asked Joe, glancing around the circle of listeners. No one responded.

"Some friend who knew you were going on this cruise must have sent it to you," Jason said.

"Some friend," Frank murmured to Joe. "With friends like that, who needs an enemy?"

"Okay, listen, people," David said. "We're going to have a great time and solve some great puzzles. And if any ghosts or curses try to stop us, they are going to be in major trouble. Right?"

"Right!" the group responded. Boris pumped his fist in the air and cheered.

"Then let's go on board," David concluded. "Find your cabins and settle in. We'll assemble on the afterdeck in half an hour for the official welcome and kickoff."

As they walked out along the pier, Joe leaned close to Frank. "I hope no one takes the word *kickoff* too seriously," he said.

The guest cabins were one level down from the main deck, along either side of a central corridor. Frank and Joe carried their packs down and studied the name tags on the doors.

Their cabin was partway along the corridor on the port side. David and Evan were on one side of them, and Elizabeth and Sylvie on the other. The cabins on the starboard side were assigned to Cesar and Jason, Boris and Kenneth, and Lisa, who somehow rated a single. Apparently Bettina was elsewhere on the boat, probably in the owner's cabin.

Once inside, Frank pushed the polished wooden door closed and dropped his bag on one of the two bunk beds. Joe wandered over to gaze out one of the two round portholes.

Frank examined the room. In one corner was a closet—in the other a bathroom, complete with a shower that was not much larger than the closet. Instead of dressers, there were latched drawers fitted under each of the beds. A table and two chairs completed the furnishings. Everything was solid and comfortable, but the decor didn't have the showiness he would have expected on a fancy yacht.

As they unpacked and stowed their clothes in the drawers, Frank and Joe talked over the day so far. Frank was curious about the encounter between Bettina and her old boss. Joe was more interested in the article about the curse on the boat. Who had sent it to Sylvie, and why? *If* someone had sent it. She could have invented that part of her story. Maybe she had found the article herself by searching a database. But if so, why would she want to hide it from the others?

Frank glanced at his watch. "We're due upstairs. Oops—I mean, on deck."

Bettina was already on the aft deck chatting with Elizabeth and Lisa. The *Teenway* editor had changed into bell-bottom jeans washed almost white, a striped fisherman's jersey, and boating shoes. Near her was a table loaded with platters of snacks and ice buckets of soft drinks. A big chocolate cake formed the centerpiece.

As the others arrived, they hovered awkwardly around the refreshment table. Frank grinned to see Evan sneak a cookie. No one else had the nerve to take something first.

Finally Bettina said, "Are we all here? Wonderful! You are a very special group, you know. You have been selected as the finest, most talented teen detectives in the country. Sherlock Holmes and Sam Spade should be happy they don't have to compete with you!"

Frank found it hard to keep a straight face. From the expressions of the listeners, most of them had no idea who the fictional detective Sam Spade was.

"Over the next few days," Bettina continued, "as we get to know these beautiful islands and one another, you'll have a chance to use your talents. I know you will find it a challenge, and I hope you will find it fun as well. So, on behalf of *Teenway* magazine, I should like to welcome all of you and wish you bon voyage and the best of luck in the contest."

As the group clapped, Bettina moved over to the table and picked up a cake knife. "Now," she said. "Who would like to be the first—"

She let out a scream and jumped back. The cake knife clattered to the deck.

Frank was the first to reach her side. "What is it?" he demanded. "Did you hurt yourself?"

Bettina pointed at the cake. Frowning, Frank moved closer.

Trapped in the chocolate frosting were four black spiders.

Gingerly, Frank picked one out. It was plastic.

"May I see that?" David asked. Frank handed it to him. David took one look and growled, "*Evan!* Front and center, on the double!"

"I didn't do anything!" Evan wailed.

"Is this yours?" his father asked.

"Maybe. It looks like one of mine," the boy admitted. "But I didn't put it on the cake. Honest."

"Did you touch the cake?" David asked.

"Well . . ." Evan licked a corner of his mouth. Frank grinned to himself. A small smudge of chocolate still showed on the boy's cheek. "I tried a little of the frosting. Just to make sure it was okay. But I did it where it wouldn't show. And I *never* put spiders on the cake. That's not funny."

"I agree," Bettina said. "It's not funny at all. Who played this unfunny joke?"

In the silence that followed, Frank heard seabirds calling and feet shuffling uneasily on the deck. Somewhere on the island, a car horn tooted.

After a long moment David said, "I believe Evan. And I want to say that to pull a stunt like this is pretty childish. But to let it be pinned on a kid— that's really low."

Bettina took a deep breath. She said, "Well—we shouldn't let some twisted soul with bad taste in jokes spoil our welcoming celebration. Who would like a piece of cake . . . with or without spiders?"

Everybody laughed, more from relief than because it was funny. David picked up the cake knife, carefully wiped it, and handed it to Bettina. She began passing out slices.

Frank didn't feel like cake. He took a plate and piled on some veggies and dip, two bite-size sandwiches, and a few cold shrimp. He paused, then added a small wedge of creamy cheese.

He was pouring a cup of soda when he noticed a man with bushy sideburns and a deep tan move down from the upper deck. The newcomer was wearing white shorts, a white short-sleeved shirt

24

with epaulets, and a blue baseball cap. He approached Bettina and murmured a few words to her.

She nodded. Then she took his arm and said, "Everyone—this is our captain, Bruce Mathieson. He tells me we'll be sailing in a few minutes. That won't break up the party, though. In fact, it gives us an additional reason to celebrate."

Mathieson returned to the upper deck. A young crew member in cutoff jeans and a Key West T-shirt came aft and took up a position near the stern mooring line. While waiting for the signal to cast off, he gazed around at the little gathering. His eyes met Frank's. Frank nodded and smiled. The crew member did not smile back or even seem to notice.

Frank had the odd impression that the guy lived in another world that just happened to run side by side with the one the *Teenway* contestants inhabited. An invisible barrier separated the two worlds. Or maybe it was just that the crew had orders not to fraternize with the passengers.

The ship's horn let out a mournful bellow. The deck began to vibrate as the huge diesel engines came to life. The crewman untied the mooring line, then looped it twice around the bollard and gripped the loose end.

The note of the engines mounted the scale. As the vibration spread and intensified, the crewman nodded to someone on the pier below. A moment later he reeled in the looped end of the mooring line. It left a sparkle of water drops on the deck.

Bettina and David left to join the captain on the bridge. David took Evan with him. Everyone else gathered by the stern rail to watch the pier and the island recede. The *Colombe d'Or* was under way.

As the boat left the sheltering arms of the bay and met the waves of the open sea, the deck began to move gently up and down and side to side. Sylvie clutched the rail and gave a small, uncomfortable laugh. "Ooo, this is fun . . . I think. Does the floor move like this always?"

"Oh, sure, always," Lisa said, giving Frank a wink. "Usually it's a lot worse than this. Don't worry, though. You'll get used to it after a few days."

"We're going to be on the boat for only a few days," Kenneth pointed out.

Lisa shrugged. "After that we can get used to being on land again."

As the laughter died down, Frank heard Elizabeth say, "I saw you hanging around the cake." He glanced over quickly. She was speaking to Cesar.

Joe had also overheard. "Is that right, Cesar?" he asked.

Cesar glared at Joe, then at Elizabeth. "None of your business," he said.

"That's original," Elizabeth said. "And it is our business. Stupid stunts like those spiders could ruin the trip for everybody."

"Okay, okay," Cesar said loudly. "Yeah, I was hanging out near the cake. I've got a thing for chocolate, all right? I was tempted to try the frosting. But I didn't do it. *And* I didn't put those dopy spiders on the cake."

"Did you notice the spiders?" Frank asked.

Cesar shook his head. "Nope. But maybe I wouldn't have. I'm a little farsighted."

"You would have noticed somebody leaning over the cake and pressing the spiders into it, wouldn't you?" Jason asked. "And you didn't, did you?"

"What's your point?" Cesar demanded.

"My point is, none of us could have put the spiders on the cake," Jason said. "The only time any of us was close enough to do it, we were all standing around looking at the refreshment table. Even a magician couldn't have sneaked those spiders past us and onto the cake."

Boris shouldered his way into the little circle and said, "They got there, though."

"Exactly," Jason said triumphantly. "Which means the solution is obvious. One of the crew put them there."

"Oh, brilliant," Boris said sarcastically. "You mean, 'The butler did it.' You've been watching too many old movies—*bad* old movies."

Jason reddened. "I suppose you've got a better solution, wise guy?"

Boris snorted loudly. "You don't have to be a cow to know when the milk tastes sour," he replied.

"Funny you should mention cows," Jason said. "After the way you horned in on this conversation."

Boris gave him a mocking smile. "At least I'm not

trying to give everyone a bum steer," he said. "I guess that's because I don't come from Cowtown."

Frank admired Boris's ready wit. How had he managed to recollect that Jason's home was Fort Worth, Texas, popularly known as Cowtown?

Jason was obviously infuriated by being topped this way. He let out a growl, lowered his head, and charged at Boris. Boris sidestepped out of his path and shouted, "Olé!"

Maddened by this additional barb, Jason swerved after Boris, but his foot slipped and he crashed into Lisa.

Lisa stumbled backward and started to topple over the rail. She let out a shriek of terror. More than a dozen feet below her was the water, churned into white foam by the powerful twin propellers.

4 Let the Games Begin!

Joe saw Lisa stumble against the rail, and he sprang into motion. Even before she began to topple over, he had narrowed the distance that separated them. With all the strength and grace he would have put into reaching out for a long pass, he grabbed her arm just above the elbow and tugged her to safety.

"You're okay," he assured her as she began to sob with mixed fright and relief. "Relax, you're fine."

Meanwhile, Frank moved quickly to Jason's side and put a friendly but warning arm around his shoulders. At first Jason seemed too shocked to react to Lisa's near fall, which he had caused. At Frank's touch, he snapped to attention. He shrugged off the arm and took a step away.

"Leave me alone," he barked.

"Hey, take it easy, fella," Frank said, moving between Jason and Boris. "We're all friends here."

"Think so?" Jason demanded. He took a couple of deep breaths and straightened his shoulders. "We'll see about that."

Not meeting anyone's eyes, he spun on one heel and stalked inside.

Lisa threw her arms around Joe's neck. "Joe Hardy, you saved my life!" she exclaimed.

Joe felt his cheeks grow warm with embarrassment. "Hey, that's okay," he muttered. He disentangled himself from her grasp. "No big deal."

"No big deal?" Lisa said. "I could have drowned or been eaten by sharks. You're a hero . . . and I'm going to make sure that every kid who reads *Teenway* knows it."

Looking past her, Joe saw that Frank was grinning. Joe's cheeks burned even more. He made a private vow. If Frank teased him about this, he was going to short-sheet Frank's bunk.

Sylvie seemed miffed by all the attention that was going to Lisa. "Are there really sharks here?" she asked with a dainty shiver.

"Sure, lots of them," Cesar said cheerfully. "But you don't have to worry about sharks as much as the jellyfish and electric eels and giant clams. Just let one of those clams get you inside its shell, and you're history!"

Elizabeth gave him a cold look. "Were you left back in tenth grade?" she asked in a haughty tone. "Or is it just your humor that's sophomoric?"

"Brrr!" Cesar said with a shiver. "I think I just hit an iceberg. Somebody get me a blanket, quick. Or better yet, a lifeboat."

Everybody laughed—everybody but Elizabeth.

Sylvie stretched and said, "It's been a long day. I think I'll rest before dinner."

"Good idea," Lisa said. "Me, too."

The two girls walked off. Boris asked, "Anybody for a game of chess? There's a board in the salon."

"Sure," Kenneth said. "I'll give it a shot."

Cesar gave Elizabeth a cheeky grin. "How about a hot game of checkers? Or maybe you know how to play fish? That kinda fits with being on a boat."

"I take back my remark about being sophomoric," Elizabeth said. "You're obviously stuck in fourth grade. Excuse me. I need to catch up on my reading."

As the girl from Virginia stalked off, Cesar looked over at Frank and Joe and rolled his eyes. "I hate stuffed shirts," he said. "Don't you?"

He didn't wait for an answer. He, too, went inside. The Hardys were left alone on deck.

"We should go have a talk with David," Joe suggested. "I'd like to make sure everything is set for tonight's crime."

"I hope there's only one," Frank replied. "The way some of these guys are getting along, we may have a murder to deal with."

Half an hour later Frank and Joe were on the sundeck near the bow with David, going over the

31

details of that evening's puzzle. The notes of a triple chime resounded through the boat.

"That must be the signal for dinner," David said, getting to his feet. "You fellows go ahead. I'd better find my kid and make sure he washes his hands."

The dark, glossy table in the forward section of the main salon glittered with china and silver for twelve. The flames of two candelabra wavered in the light breeze from the deck.

Everyone waited near the entrance for somebody to go in first.

Bettina came in and stood near the head of the table. She had changed again—this time into a light green dress decorated with sea horses and anchors. "Please sit anywhere you like," she said. "We're going to be quite informal."

Cesar eyed the table. In a loud whisper he said, "If this is 'quite informal,' I sure hope she doesn't decide to get formal. I left my white tie and tails back in Albuquerque."

Sylvie went to a seat halfway along the far side of the table. Jason and Boris rushed over to grab the chairs on either side of her, then glared at each other.

Lisa came up to Joe. "May I sit next to you?" she asked sweetly. "I want to hear all about the mysteries you've solved."

Frank gave Joe an amused look. Joe wrinkled his nose at him.

Elizabeth took the seat next to David and asked him his views on the future of the American theater. From his expression, David would probably have rather been discussing the NCAA Final Four.

The first course was a salad with asparagus stalks and orange slices. The look Evan gave it cracked Joe up.

Everyone ate the salad in a tense and uneasy silence. Joe decided the problem was mostly the formality of the dinner table, but the tensions between some of the contestants didn't help the atmosphere.

The only one who seemed totally unaffected by the atmosphere was Evan. After eating his orange slices and sliding his asparagus under a convenient lettuce leaf, he looked around and said, "I know a riddle."

"Evan . . ." David said in a warning tone.

"What's your riddle?" Joe asked.

Evan took a deep breath. "Why did the boy throw his alarm clock out the window?"

Joe put on a very thoughtful expression. "Um, let's see . . . Because it went off too early and he didn't want to wake up yet?" he suggested.

Before Evan could respond to this, Elizabeth said, "Don't be ridiculous. Because he wanted to make time fly, of course."

"That's right," Evan said, crestfallen. "Wait, wait—I've got another one. How many balls of string would it take to reach to the moon?"

Not allowing enough time for anyone to speak, he said, "Give up? One, if it's big enough."

That got a chorus of groans from around the

33

table. Encouraged by the response, Evan continued. "Here's a good one. Where did Napoleon keep his armies?"

"In France?" Jason said.

"No, no," Boris cut in. "In Russia. You know what happened to Napoleon. Once his armies went to Russia, they never returned."

"You're both wrong." Evan chortled. "You know where Napoleon kept his armies? *In his sleevies!*"

After dinner Frank and David went to put the final touches on the first mystery. Joe stayed with the contestants in the salon. No one talked. Sylvie sat on the couch with a magazine open on her lap, never turning a single page. Boris paced around the room, pausing now and then to stare out at the darkness. The others simply sat, gazing vacantly into space. Joe decided they must be psyching themselves for the contest.

David and Frank returned. David was holding a baseball cap upside down.

"I've put five numbered slips of paper in here," he announced. "You'll each take one to determine the order of play."

He went around the room. Jason drew number one, followed by Cesar, Sylvie, Boris, and Elizabeth.

"Joe will take each of you in turn to the scene of the crime," David continued. "You'll have five minutes to look around. Don't touch anything. Afterward you'll fill out a report explaining your interpretation of the crime, the culprit or culprits, and the evidence. Your score will be based on how close you come to the official version . . . in other words, mine."

That drew a slight, nervous laugh from everyone.

"Okay, let's go," David concluded. "And may the best detective win!"

Joe led Jason out of the salon and up a flight of stairs to a door marked Private.

"This is the captain's cabin," he explained. "As background, you should know that the yacht's owner asked the captain to keep a file of securities in his safe. Their value is over a million dollars."

"I can guess what comes next," Jason said.

Joe didn't reply. He pushed the door open and stood aside. He glanced at his watch. Then he followed Jason into the cabin.

The first thing he noticed was a body sprawled on the floor in front of the open safe. It was dressed in oil-stained khakis and work boots. A length of electric cord was knotted around the neck.

"That's a dummy, right?" Jason asked. His voice quavered.

"Right," Joe said. "And that is the only question I'm allowed to answer. Your five minutes started fifteen seconds ago."

Jason set to work. He studied the dummy from head to foot, then peered into the safe. The papers spilled on the rug occupied him for a minute or more. Then he moved around the cabin. He looked closely at the files on the desk and the overturned glass on the end table. A wrench half-tucked into a chair cushion didn't seem to interest him. He spent what was left of his five minutes getting down on his hands and knees to sniff the barrel of a snub-nosed .38 revolver peeping out from under the dummy's leg.

"Time," Joe announced. He escorted Jason back to the salon and returned with Cesar. Unlike Jason, Cesar kept up a running stream of comments as he examined the crime scene. Some of them were to the point. Others were so wacky that Joe had to work not to laugh.

Each of the other contestants also had a different style. Sylvie acted like an airhead, but she noticed as many important details as anyone else. Boris spent the first half of his time posed just inside the doorway. Only his eyes moved. Then he went around the cabin counterclockwise, pausing to check each clue in turn. As for Elizabeth, she stood as if she were there for a social engagement with the captain. Joe half expected her to send him off for tea and pastries.

After all the contestants had had their turns, they were given half an hour to complete their crime reports. Frank and Joe collected the five papers and took them to their cabin. Frank stuck the folder inside his suitcase for safekeeping. Then they returned to the salon. They expected that the others would want to party on their first night at sea, but the only one still there was Lisa.

"Everybody pooped out," Lisa told them. "It *has* been a pretty long day. But how could anyone give up the chance to watch the moon rise over the water?"

"When does it rise tonight?" Joe asked.

"Oh, I don't know," Lisa admitted. "But it has to come up sooner or later. Why don't we just go out on deck and wait for it?"

Pointedly, Frank picked up a magazine and sat down on one of the two leather sofas.

"You promised to tell me about some of your cases," Lisa added. "For my *Teenway* story."

Joe didn't recall making such a promise, but it was a reasonable request. He went out on the afterdeck with Lisa and told her about the time he and Frank had gone undercover as actors in a Broadway musical. It took a while. When he finished, he looked around. The moon still wasn't up. Or had it already set?

"I'd better turn in," he said, getting to his feet. "Big day tomorrow."

He said good night to Lisa and collected Frank from the salon. As they went down to their cabin, Joe noticed a line of light across the floor coming from the door to their cabin.

"Frank!" Joe whispered urgently. He grabbed his brother's arm. "We didn't leave the door open or the light on. Somebody has been in our cabin!"

5 Shutting the Barn Door

Frank instantly flattened himself against the wall on the near side of the door. Wordlessly he pointed to the far side of the door. Joe nodded and moved silently into position.

Frank took a deep breath and held up his left hand with three fingers showing. As he folded them, he counted down under his breath.

Three . . . two . . . one . . .

On zero, he shoved the door open, darted through the opening, and dodged to the right. He finished in a martial crouch, hands poised for either offense or defense.

At the same time Joe sprinted inside and took up a position to the left of the door.

Frank quickly scanned the room. No one was there. He jerked open the closet door. At the same moment, Joe pulled open the door to the bathroom and peered inside.

Frank straightened up. "All clear," he said, shutting the closet. He stepped over and eased the door to the corridor closed.

"Frank, look at this," Joe said. He pointed to Frank's suitcase. It was unzipped. The folder of questionnaires lay on the floor next to it.

Frank started to bend down to retrieve the folder. Then he stopped himself.

"This doesn't make sense," he said.

"Sure it does," Joe said. "One of the contestants decided to improve his or her chances by changing their entry . . . or by changing other people's entries."

"That's what we're supposed to think," Frank replied. "But if that's so, why was the folder left where we'd see it and know that someone had fiddled with it? Why were the lights on and the door open?"

"Nervousness?" Joe suggested. "Somebody came along before the intruder could put things back?"

Frank considered that and nodded slowly. "It's possible," he said. "I'm not sold. I have a strong hunch this is some kind of setup. But what kind, and why? See if you spot anything else."

While Joe circled the cabin, Frank checked the crime reports. Had any been altered? Each of the contestants had made some changes in what he or she had written. As far as Frank could see, however, the insertions and crossings out were done in the same ink as the rest of the entry. There were no obvious signs of tampering.

"Frank?" Joe said. "Come here a sec."

Frank stood up and crossed the cabin to where Joe was standing.

"Sniff," Joe told him.

Frank sniffed. "I smell something flowery," he reported. "Perfume?"

"I think so," Joe replied. "And I think I smelled it before, earlier today. Sylvie was wearing it. She must be the one who came in here."

Frank frowned. The thought of Sylvie playing burglar surprised him. His experience as a detective had taught him not to rule out suspects simply because they "weren't the type." Still, some people were more likely to carry out certain kinds of actions than others. Sylvie did not strike him as being very adventurous or daring.

Frank looked around. Set into the wall above Joe's bunk was the rectangular metal grill of a ventilator. On the other side of that wall was the cabin shared by Elizabeth and Sylvie. Could the scent have seeped in through the duct? And if so, what about sound? Could the girls hear what he and Joe said?

They had better be more careful about where they discussed anything sensitive. Frank tapped Joe on the shoulder, put a finger to his lips, and pointed up at the ventilator. Joe nodded grimly. Grabbing a pen and a piece of paper, he scribbled, "Tell David? Bettina?"

Frank glanced at his watch and shook his head. "Not now, it's too late," he said in a low voice. "We'll catch them first thing in the morning. This isn't news they'll want to hear."

Frank's prediction was right. Early the next morning he and Joe knocked on the door to David's cabin. Still in pajamas, he listened to their account of the intrusion. His expression grew more and more unhappy.

When the Hardys finished, David said, "We'd better let Bettina in on this. Just a minute while I throw some clothes on."

Once dressed, David took Frank and Joe up to the main deck, to the owner's cabin. It ran the full width of the yacht, with big windows facing the bow and both sides. There they repeated their story to Bettina.

She looked over the folder of entries. "Let me be sure I understand," she said. "Someone may have altered one or more of these, but you can't tell whether or not, or which one. Is that it?"

"'Fraid so," Frank said. "If only we'd looked at the papers when the contestants turned them in . . ."

"Spilt milk," Bettina said, with a wave of the hand. "So—what do we do about last night's mystery? Keep it? Scrub it?"

"I looked over the entries last night," Frank said. "They're all pretty good, but I didn't see any that seemed outstandingly good . . . or bad. My guess is that they would all earn roughly the same score."

"In other words," Joe added, "whether we keep the first puzzle or drop it won't make that much difference to the final result."

"Hmm . . . I'd rather not cloud the contest with unnecessary controversy," Bettina remarked. "David? Any thoughts?"

"I see two possibilities," David said slowly. "One, somebody improved his own entry. Two, somebody sabotaged someone else's entry. Or both possibilities, of course."

"Okay," Bettina said. "What then?"

"I'm not sure how we could prove or disprove the first possibility," David continued. "But the second should be easy to check. We post all the entries for the contestants to look over. Then we listen for anyone's complaining that someone changed his entry. If we get any complaints, we decide then whether to honor the results. If we don't, we let it ride."

"And we'll be a lot more careful from now on," Frank said.

"Good point, Frank," Bettina said. "How are we going to secure the contest materials in the future?"

"How about the captain's safe?" Joe suggested. "I hear he's in the habit of keeping millions in securities there. A few contest entries should be a cinch."

After a startled moment, the others laughed.

"Sorry, you can't use that safe," Bettina said. "The combination was lost years ago. Any other ideas?"

"I have a file box in my cabin that locks," David offered. "You'd need a certain degree of skill to open it, and I doubt if anybody would have the nerve to make off with the whole file box."

Bettina gave a decisive nod. "All right, then," she said. "David, take these entries and score them. We're scheduled to reach Fort William early this afternoon. While we're docked, have someone make a couple of sets of photocopies. Then keep the originals locked in that file box of yours."

"Will do," David responded. "Should we announce the scores this morning, as scheduled?"

"We should do everything as normally as possible," Bettina told him. She stood up. "If someone hopes to disrupt our contest, we should make it obvious that it isn't working. That may drive him or her to make a mistake."

The Hardys returned to David's cabin with him. He showed them the file box, and Frank checked the lock. It seemed pretty sturdy.

"I'm going up to the sundeck to do the scoring," David announced. "It's very private at this time of day. Don't worry, I won't let the entries blow away. And the minute I finish—it shouldn't take long—I'll bring them back down here until we post them later. They'll be safe, I guarantee it."

The three left together. As Frank and Joe walked down the corridor to their cabin, Joe was startled to see the door to David's cabin start to open.

Evan walked out. "Oh, hi, Joe," the boy said. "Is it time to eat yet? I'm starved."

"Er—just about," Joe replied. His thoughts whirled. Evan had obviously been inside the room earlier, too. Where, in the shower? Had he overheard their conversation with his dad? And if so, should Joe warn him not to mention anything he'd heard to anyone else?

Maybe not—that might put ideas in the kid's head.

"You want to wait for us?" Joe added. "We're about to go up, too."

A breakfast buffet was set up in the dining area. Boris, Jason, and Lisa were already eating. Sylvie was waiting for Cesar to finish filling his plate. Frank, Joe, and Evan lined up behind her.

"We are all arguing about last night's mystery puzzle," Sylvie told Joe and Frank. "Will you end our suspense? Please?"

"That's David's job," Frank replied. "Don't worry—he'll be along pretty soon."

Sylvie poured a glass of orange juice and fixed a bowl of granola with fresh tropical fruit on top. Evan was more interested in the miniature pastries. He took three and reached for another, then glanced up at Joe and took a glass of milk instead.

Joe and Frank each took a slice of fresh mango, scrambled eggs, and portions of an unusual looking sausage. They joined the others at the table.

Jason looked over at them. "The guy was the robber's inside man, right?" he said. "He and his boss got into an argument and the boss offed him."

"No comment," Joe replied.

"That's totally dumb," Cesar told Jason. He noticed Kenneth aiming his camera at him and paused to put on a big smile. Kenneth did not snap the shutter. After a moment Cesar dropped the smile and continued. "What about the ransom note? How do you explain that?"

"What ransom note?" Boris demanded. "There was no kidnapping."

Cesar stuck one finger in the air. "Aha!" he said. "No kidnapping—but there *was* a ransom note."

From the entrance, Elizabeth remarked, "These airs of mystery are so tiresome and passé. Not to mention childish."

With a wide grin, Cesar held his thumbs to his ears and waggled his fingers at her. Elizabeth put her nose in the air and sniffed loudly. Kenneth's flash went off.

"Oh!" Elizabeth exploded. "You had better not print that picture in the magazine! If my daddy saw it, he'd sue you and *Teenway* for all you're worth."

"Quick, somebody hold me," Cesar cried. "I'm trembling so much I can't stand up."

"You're sitting down," Boris pointed out.

"You see? That's how bad it is!" Cesar replied.

Joe noticed that Lisa was holding her tape recorder just below the level of the table. She pointed the built-in mike at each speaker in turn.

As Elizabeth came nearer the table, she spotted Lisa's recorder. "Is that thing on?" she demanded. "I want that tape!"

"You can order a copy from me when I get back to New York," Lisa said coolly. "My rates are pretty reasonable."

"I don't know anything worse than a dirty little snoop!" Elizabeth declared.

"Ooo—major diss!" Cesar said, snickering.

Lisa reddened. "I know something a lot worse than a snoop, and that's a snob!"

"Hey, come on, people," Frank said. "Lighten up."

He might as well have saved his breath.

"I refuse to be called names!" Elizabeth cried.

"Who started calling names?" Lisa retorted. She shoved her chair back and sprang to her feet. "Who started it?"

"Are we doing more riddles?" Evan asked eagerly. "'Cause I remembered some good ones."

Joe patted him on the arm. "Not now, Evan," he said in an undertone. "Eat your breakfast."

Elizabeth put her hands on her hips and glared at

Lisa. She opened her mouth to make another remark. Before she got a word out, she was interrupted by a distant, startled cry. Elizabeth looked over her shoulder toward the companionway, or stairway, to the cabin deck. At that moment there was a loud crash from below.

6 Slipping and Sliding

Frank jumped up from the table and darted toward the stairs. Joe was close behind him. As they zoomed down the steps, Frank saw one of the crew running along the corridor. The door to David's cabin was open wide. The crew member started inside.

"Wha—" he yelled. His feet flew out from under him. He landed flat on his back with a crash that shook the deck.

Frank stopped and held out his arm to warn Joe. They approached the doorway slowly and cautiously.

David was sitting on the floor of the cabin, just inside the door. He had a blue-and-white marble in his hand. Frank saw dozens more marbles scattered across the polished planks.

The crew member sat up. Frank recognized him.

He had handled the mooring line during their departure the day before. "Woo!" he said, rubbing the back of his head. "What hit me?"

"You slipped on a marble," David told him. "Sorry about that, ah—what was your name again?"

"Chuck . . . Chuck Arneson," the guy replied. "We'd better pick these up before somebody cracks their skull. How'd they spill anyway?"

"I can make a pretty good guess," David said. He got to his feet and massaged his hip.

From behind Frank and Joe, a tiny voice said, "Daddy? I have something to tell you."

David sighed. "Yes, Evan? What is it?"

Evan slipped past Frank and Joe. "Well . . . I heard you and Frank and Joe talking about robbers," he said. "And I was afraid a bad guy would come in our room. So I put my marbles on the floor to make him fall."

"It worked," David said with grim humor.

"I would have told you," Evan continued. "But I didn't know where you were. And then I went up to breakfast and I sort of forgot. I'm sorry. Are you okay?"

"I'm fine," David said. He reached over and tousled his son's hair. "But next time, check with me before you set any traps for bad guys. Okay?"

Evan grinned with relief. "You bet!"

Frank and Joe helped pick up the marbles. Then they returned to the salon with David and Evan. David carried an envelope in his hand. The room fell silent as they went in.

"I've looked over your solutions to last night's crime," David announced. "They are all worthy tries. I'm going to post them on the bulletin board next to the stairs for you to read. Then, in ten or fifteen minutes, we'll come together again to talk about the results."

The five finalists barely waited for David to tack up the entries before they clustered around to read them. Meanwhile, Lisa cornered Joe. She wanted to know what the commotion had been about earlier. He told her about Evan's marbles. She asked for a preview of the scores in the contest. Joe admitted he had no idea.

Lisa wanted his general reactions to the voyage so far. Joe talked about the boat, the sea, the weather, and the great group of contestants. He aimed his words at Lisa's tape recorder. In his head, however, he was focused on the mystery of the intruder from the night before. Finally he muttered an excuse and went to look for Frank. He found him on the afterdeck.

"Notice anything?" Frank murmured. "No anguished cries from anyone whose entry was altered."

"So either nothing was changed or our visitor last night came to touch up his own entry," Joe replied.

Frank nodded. "That's what it looks like. Unless . . . I can't stop thinking we were *meant* to notice that someone had fiddled with the entries. But why?"

Joe had the feeling an answer to Frank's question was lurking just out of sight. Suddenly he snapped his fingers. "How about this? One of the contestants was sure he'd messed up. So he decided to push us into throwing out the results. That way his poor showing wouldn't hurt him. Or her, of course."

"That fits," Frank said slowly. "The funny part is, from what David said, everybody did about the same. So breaking into our cabin was wasted effort."

"But whoever did it couldn't have known that." Joe glanced inside. "Speaking of David, it looks like he's ready to start."

Joe and Frank returned to the salon. David gave them a nod and a smile. Then he said, "The setup last night was meant to suggest that one of the crew, an engineer, interrupted a burglar who killed him to stop him from raising an alarm. That was a false trail. None of you fell for it."

"The knot was toward the front," Boris said. "The victim must have been facing his attacker. How do you get a cord around somebody's neck from the front unless he knows you?"

"And the gun," Sylvie said. "If I were the criminal and somebody discovered me, I would shoot him. I would not hope to find a piece of electrical cord to strangle him with."

Joe was tempted to point out that guns make more noise than strangling cords. He restrained himself. This was David's show.

"A quarrel among thieves," Cesar remarked. "But what about the ransom note? I spotted it under the chair. It offered to return the bonds for a quarter of a million dollars. Why would thieves do that?"

"Maybe the bonds are too hard to cash," Jason suggested. "You know—like counterfeiters who sell their phony bills for a few cents on the dollar."

"Cesar is the only one who mentioned the ransom note," David announced. "There's another detail none of you picked up on—the victim's hands."

"What about them?" Sylvie asked, puzzled.

"Wait, wait!" Cesar shouted. He slapped the table. "Of course! The hands were clean, and the nails were manicured. That was no engineer. An engineer would have oily hands and cracked nails. I bet that was the owner of the yacht. He was planning to steal his own bonds, then rip off the insurance company for the ransom! He probably gave the crew the evening off, to get them out of the way. But one of them suspected something and stayed behind."

"Bravo, Cesar," David said. "You got it."

"Yeah," Cesar groaned. "I got it today—but not last night, when it would have done me some good."

"Then the killer was the real engineer, right?" Boris asked. "He changed clothes with the victim to confuse the authorities while he made his escape."

"He certainly confused me." Sylvie laughed.

A general discussion broke out. Joe and Frank joined in. So did Lisa and even Kenneth. The only one who kept out of it was Elizabeth. Her expression and body language said she found the whole business childish. Joe wondered why she had entered the contest if that was how she felt. Here was still another puzzle to be solved.

The second part of the detective contest took place toward the end of the morning. It was a test of observational skills. Everyone gathered around the TV to watch a tape.

Like the contestants, Frank and Joe watched intently. On the screen, a man and two women met on a street corner. They chatted for a few moments. Two other men approached from opposite directions. One of them bumped into the woman on the left. He muttered an apology and walked away.

A moment later the woman he had collided with groped in her purse and let out a shriek. The man who was talking with her ran after the one who had bumped her. At that, the tape ended.

David stood up and passed out questionnaires to the contestants. "Okay," he said. "No conversation until all of you have finished your responses."

Joe took a spare questionnaire from David and gave it a shot. It was not easy. The questions included the clothing and personal appearance of all five people in the scene, what each had said, and exactly what had happened.

David collected the completed questionnaires and put them in a manila envelope. "Okay—any remarks?"

"This is kid stuff," Elizabeth said. "I'm not saying I remembered all those stupid details. Who could? But the important part was simply babyish."

"Wa-a-ah!" Cesar said with a grin. Elizabeth sniffed loudly and looked in the other direction.

"The important part being . . . ?" David asked, looking around the circle.

"The guy stole her wallet when he shoved her," Jason said. "That's an old stunt. Some dude tried it on me once when I was getting off a bus. I gave him a swift elbow below the belt. Boy, did he look surprised."

"What do you think happened after the tape ended?" David asked.

Boris shrugged. "The other guy—the woman's friend—probably caught him. He was pretty fast off the mark."

"And then?" David continued.

"The police put the pickpocket in jail," Sylvie said.

"Maybe it works that way in Canada," Cesar said. "My bet is he got himself a terrific lawyer and walked."

"So, Sylvie, you think the perpetrator was arrested. What about the rest of you? Everybody agree?" David asked, giving another look around the circle. The contestants nodded.

"Joe? Frank?" David added.

"Well . . ." Frank said. He glanced over at Joe, who gave him a grin. "Tell them."

"Even if the pickpocket got caught," Joe said, "I doubt if the cops could arrest him. No evidence."

"What about the wallet?" Elizabeth demanded. "Even if he threw it down on the sidewalk, it would still tell against him."

"He didn't have the wallet," Frank said. "Right after he took it, he passed it to his accomplice, who strolled off in the other direction. Right, David?"

"I *knew* there was something about that other guy," Cesar said. He slapped his palm against his forehead.

"You tricked us!" Elizabeth declared crossly.

David smiled. "Good," he said. "I was hoping to. Just remember, the bad guys aren't out to make it easy for crime solvers."

Lunch was assorted sandwiches and chips, served on the afterdeck. No one would have wanted to stay inside and miss the view. The *Colombe d'Or* was approaching its next port of call. Ahead, a green island loomed up out of the blue sea. Frank thought its steep slopes and peak looked like a child's drawing of a volcano.

David confirmed this. "That's Mount Orange," he told the group. "It's still active. The last major eruption was about fifty years ago. It buried one of the towns on the island under superheated gas and ash. Over ten thousand people died."

Sylvie shivered. "That's terrible! What if it explodes while we are there?"

"There's usually some warning before a big eruption," Frank assured her. "Sort of like clearing your throat before you sing."

"In any case," David added, "we'll dock at Fort William. The volcano has never touched it. The town that was destroyed was on the opposite side of the island. If we had more time, we could go over and explore the ruins."

"Spooky-y-y," Cesar said in a hollow voice. He waved his open hands in Sylvie's direction.

"Ooo, don't!" Sylvie exclaimed. Cesar grinned.

"Let her alone," Boris said gruffly.

"Yeah, stop playing the clown," Jason added.

Cesar's grin flickered. "At least I know when I act like a clown," he retorted. "Unlike some people I could name who don't know it and can't help it."

Sylvie smiled at him. "It's all right, Cesar," she said. "I know you were just trying to be funny. I think you're cute."

Cesar beamed. Frank glanced at Jason and Boris. Both were trying to look unconcerned.

"How long will we be stuck on this island?" Elizabeth asked in a bored voice. "Is there anything to do on it?"

"The old part of the city is very picturesque," David replied. "I like to just wander. There are also some very elegant boutiques and shops around the square."

Elizabeth's face brightened.

The boat docked alongside a palm-lined boulevard. Nearby, Frank spotted the colorful umbrellas of an outdoor café. From the harbor, the old town rose in level after level of white-stone buildings with lacy iron balconies and red-tile roofs. The green slopes of Mount Orange supplied a lush backdrop.

Frank and Joe stood at the rail admiring the view. "Do you think they have a college here?" Joe wondered out loud. "I could handle four years in a place like this."

"Huh," Frank replied. "You'd probably spend your four years lying on the beach waiting for a nice ripe guava to plop into your mouth."

Joe smiled. "You could do worse. But I like mangoes better." He lowered his voice and added, "We should try to keep an eye on everyone while we're ashore this afternoon. Why don't I concentrate on Sylvie? That was her perfume in our room last night."

"Good idea," Frank said. "And I'll watch Elizabeth. There's something I don't get about her attitude."

"*Attitude*'s the word," Joe said, rolling his eyes. "That girl is nothing *but* attitude!"

As the teens left the boat, David warned them to be back by four o'clock. "Have a great time," he added. "If you need to get in touch, you have the telephone number here. Bettina and I will both be on board."

The group stayed together just long enough to

reach the first corner. Sylvie eyed the narrow cobbled street that twisted its way uphill under lines hung with brightly colored wash.

"Let's go this way," she eagerly urged. "I bet we'll find some awesome views up the hill."

Elizabeth sniffed. "A slum's a slum," she said. "Even in the Caribbean. I'd rather find the square and check out the shops."

"Okay. Have fun," Sylvie said with a touch of sarcasm in her tone. She started up the little street. After a moment's hesitation the others followed. Only Frank stayed behind. Elizabeth bit her lower lip as she watched the group walk away. Then she tossed her blond hair in a way that was meant to say, "Why should I care about *them*?"

"I detest sight-seeing," Elizabeth told Frank. "It's so boring. Our place in Virginia is just a mile from a Civil War battleground. One of my daddy's relatives commanded a battalion there. But I've never visited. I can't stand all those noisy, smelly charter buses. And the people with their camcorders! Sometimes they walk right up to our house and take each other's pictures on our front porch. Can you imagine?"

Frank started to say, "Maybe you should charge admission." He thought better of it.

Elizabeth didn't notice. "I really thought there would be more people like me on this cruise. After all, a yacht in the Caribbean . . . I didn't stop to think that a magazine like *Teenway* has to appeal to

58

a pretty mixed bag. I do wish the others didn't resent me for my advantages, though. I can't help who I am or who my ancestors were, can I?"

Frank was tempted to say that she might try not acting so stuck-up. He decided to keep his mouth shut. After all, he was a detective, not an advice columnist.

By three-thirty Joe was ready to bang his head against a wall. While sticking close to Sylvie, he was also trying to keep track of everyone else in his group. But how could he? All afternoon they kept wandering off, hanging back, dawdling in shops, hurrying ahead. It was as if they had all secretly decided to drive him bonkers!

Now he was in a tiny square where five alleys— they were too narrow to be called streets—met. Against one of the house walls, a stone fountain burbled. Cesar held his cupped hands under the stream of water.

"Don't drink that," Sylvie warned. "You might catch something."

Instead of drinking, Cesar poured the water over his head. "Ah! That's better," he said. He looked around. "Where is everybody?"

"Off," Sylvie replied with a vague wave of the hand. "It's late. We should get back to the yacht."

"How? Jason's the only one who can find his way around this place," Cesar said. "He's amazing."

As if summoned, Jason appeared. "We're late,"

he said. He pointed down one of the alleys. To Joe it looked no different from the others. "That should be the shortest way back."

As they walked downhill, the others joined them. Soon they emerged from the clustered houses at the seafront boulevard, just across from where the yacht was moored. At that moment Frank and Elizabeth came along. Elizabeth was carrying a shopping bag with the linked initials of a famous French designer. Joe caught Frank's eye. Frank shrugged.

The group started across the boulevard. Suddenly four motorbikes sped out of a side street and cut right in front of them. Each motorbike had a big metal box on the back, emblazoned with the words "All-Island Pizza. We D-liver, You D-light." The riders halted next to the gangplank of the *Colombe d'Or*.

"Hey, hey, hey," Boris said. "Looks like we eat pizza tonight. That's a nice surprise."

The four riders took stacks of cardboard boxes from the carriers and started toward the boat. A man in a double-breasted white chef's jacket met them and kept them from going aboard.

"NO!" he shouted as the teens drew closer. "No one ordered pizzas. If we want pizza, *I* make pizza!"

"Somebody ordered fifteen pies," one of the riders insisted. He held out a slip of paper. "Here, see? The name of the boat, fifteen pies, plain, mushrooms, extra cheese . . . it's all here."

"It must be a joke," the chef said. "I tell you, we did not order pizza."

"Some joke! What do we do with fifteen pies?" the deliveryman demanded.

From the upper deck, Bettina said, "It's all right. We'll accept them. Arnie, pay him—and be sure to include a generous tip."

"Yes, ma'am," the chef said in a grumpy tone.

"The prankster strikes again," Joe murmured to Frank. "We'd better—"

Nearby, voices were suddenly raised. "Come on, admit it!" Jason said to Boris. "I saw you sneak into that shop and make a phone call. And I overheard you say the name of the yacht."

"Big deal," Boris said. "That proves nothing."

Jason stuck out his chin. "You want proof? I heard more than that. I heard you when you said *mushrooms* and *cheese!*"

7 A Telltale Chime

Everyone clustered around Boris and Jason. From her position on the boat, Bettina heard Jason's accusation and came ashore to join the group.

"What about it, Boris?" Cesar asked. "Did you really call in that order for pizza?"

"It is not a very funny joke," Sylvie said.

Frank studied Boris's expression. He did not look flustered by the pressure. If anything, there was a hint of secret amusement. What was the joke—if not the pizzas themselves?

"Yes, I made a phone call," Boris announced.

"Really, Boris, this sort of prank—" Bettina started to say.

Boris interrupted her. "But I did not call a pizzeria. I called a friend back home. Her name is

Christina. If you want to check with her, I will give you her number."

"I heard you say the *Colombe d'Or*," Jason repeated.

Boris shrugged. "I was bragging about being on a fancy yacht. I told her the name of the yacht."

"Okay, but what about the mushrooms and cheese?" Joe asked.

"I told Christina that tensions were mushrooming among us," Boris replied. He smiled. "And—please excuse it, Bettina—I think I called you the Big Cheese."

"I don't mind," Bettina said. "As an editor, I've been called a lot worse."

Boris turned to Jason. "Satisfied?" he demanded belligerently. "Or did you maybe also hear me say something about anchovies?"

Everybody cracked up, except Jason, who turned away with a resentful expression.

"Hey, everybody, let's get with it," Cesar said. "All those pizzas are getting cold!"

The group boarded the yacht. Arnie, the chef and steward, had already set up a table on the afterdeck with plates, napkins, and cold drinks. As they filed back, he and Chuck, the crew member who had slipped on Evan's marbles that morning, appeared with four steaming pizzas, two plain and two with mushrooms. No anchovies, as Boris pointed out.

Frank and Joe each took a slice of pizza. Frank chose plain and Joe chose mushroom. They went to a corner of the deck where they couldn't be overheard.

"Our prankster seems to be getting more ambitious," Frank said. "First it's plastic spiders in the cake, now a lifetime supply of pizzas."

"Don't forget David's runaway laptop," Joe replied. "Not to mention entering our room and rifling the contest entries."

Frank nodded. "The thing is, we had no real leads until now. This is different. There's a good chance the trickster left a trail. Let's check it out. What was the name of that pizzeria?"

"All-Island, I think," Joe told him. "Anyway, how many can there be in a town this size?"

When the boat was at sea, the telephone for passengers worked via a satellite dish, but when the boat docked, the phone was hooked up to a landline.

Frank got the number of the pizzeria and dialed. A man answered. When Frank explained what he wanted, the man passed the phone to a woman with a Caribbean lilt in her voice.

"Oh, yes, I remember," she said. "I will not so easily forget an order for fifteen pies, and that a false one, too!"

"What can you tell me about the person who called?" Frank asked.

"Not so very much," she replied. "The voice was muffled. It was high for a man but low for a woman. A Yankee accent, I think. Like yours."

"Didn't it surprise you, getting such a big order

from a stranger? Weren't you suspicious?" Frank wondered.

"From now on I will be," the woman said with a musical laugh. "But we are used to orders from yachts for delivery to dockside. This is the first time we have a problem."

"I see," Frank said. "Do you happen to know what time the call came in?"

"Oh, yes, just before three-thirty," the woman told him.

"How sure are you?" Frank probed. "Did you write down the time?"

"No, but the caller asked us to deliver at precisely four," she replied. "I checked my watch to see if we could do it. Just then I heard a clock chime the half hour."

Puzzled, Frank asked, "A clock chimed? From a building near you, you mean?"

"No, no, I heard the sound over the telephone," the woman explained.

Frank glanced around. A few feet away, hanging on the wall, was an old-fashioned chiming clock. The hands indicated four forty-four. The second hand was just passing the halfway point.

Quickly, Frank said into the phone, "Please listen." He pointed the handset at the clock.

Bing bang bing bong . . .

The sound died away. He put the receiver to his ear. "Well?" he asked.

"That is exactly the same sound," the woman said. "But another clock might sound the same, too.

My auntie has one with chimes like that. I'm sorry. I wish I could help more."

"You've helped a lot," Frank assured her. "Thank you."

He hung up and told Joe what he had learned.

Joe stared at him. "But, Frank . . . you see what that means? If she heard this clock, then whoever made the call had to be on the boat at three-thirty."

"Right," Frank said.

Joe frowned. "I couldn't keep everyone in sight the whole time," he admitted. "But I don't see how anyone could have made it back here, placed the call, and got back up the hill without me noticing."

"And I was with Elizabeth the whole time," Frank said. "I think I deserve a bonus for that, by the way. Talk about a hardship assignment. So in other words, we can eliminate everyone . . . except David, Bettina, and the crew."

"And Evan," Joe pointed out. "Joke. Wait a minute, though. Kenneth *did* come back to the boat. He needed to get more film. Do you suppose he . . . ?"

"He's the most unlikely suspect," Frank pointed out. "But it's only in books that the most unlikely suspect is always the one who did it. In real life, it's usually the most *likely* suspect who's guilty. Still, maybe Kenneth saw something while he was here. We should ask him."

"Sure," Joe said. "But I think we should focus more on motive. Somebody wants to mess up this voyage. That's pretty clear. But why? How much do we really know about any of these people?"

"Not enough, obviously," Frank replied. "Let's go mingle and find out more."

The others were still on the afterdeck, enjoying the late afternoon sun and the fresh breeze from the sea. Lisa was seated near the rail with a can of soda in her hand. She saw Joe arrive and waved. He hesitated, then went over to join her. As a writer, she might have noticed something useful.

"Hey, Joe. Have you unmasked the pizza maniac?" Lisa asked.

Joe dragged over a chair and sat down. "Not yet. Any helpful hints?"

Lisa looked thoughtful. "Boris ate three slices with mushrooms," she said. "I'd call that a clue, wouldn't you?"

"A clue to his appetite, sure," Joe replied with a grin. "No, seriously—any idea why somebody would want to wreck the contest?"

Lisa stared out over the water. "It's a mystery," she said at last. "This contest means a lot to them. Not just getting to spend a few days living like a millionaire. Though I'm not putting that down. I like it. I could get used to it."

"Me, too," Joe assured her.

"Take Cesar," Lisa continued. "His grandparents immigrated from Mexico. His dad is an auto mechanic and his mom works in a dry cleaner's. He's got an older sister and two younger brothers. Winning this contest is his one big chance to be able to go away to a really good college. Do you think he's going to ruin that with some dumb stunts?"

"I see your point," Joe said. "How do you know so much about Cesar?"

Lisa smiled. "I asked. Most people love to talk about themselves. I love to listen to them. It's a perfect match."

It's different with me, Joe thought ruefully. When people know they're talking to a detective, they always watch what they say, even the ones who don't have anything to hide.

"Boris, too," Lisa said. "Back in Russia, his mother was a doctor and his father was an engineer. Now they run a little grocery store in Brooklyn. Boris will do okay whatever happens, but winning the *Teenway* scholarship would give him a big head start. Why would he want to blow that?"

"What about Elizabeth?" Joe asked. "She doesn't act as if she needs a college scholarship."

Lisa rolled her eyes. "Elizabeth's really not so bad when she forgets she's one of the Virginia Wheelwrights," she said. "The problem is, that doesn't happen very often."

Joe chuckled. "So who's left? Jason and Sylvie."

"I can't figure Jason," Lisa said, shaking her head. "One minute I think he's really sharp. The next minute I can't believe there's anything in his mind more complicated than deciding which side of his nose to pierce next. As for Sylvie, don't get me started. Either she's exactly the bubblehead she appears to be, or she is so deep it's scary."

68

"Whatever, it's hard to see what their motives might be," Joe said.

"Maybe we're looking too hard," Lisa suggested. "What if these stunts are just pure malicious mischief? What if somebody simply likes to watch the rest of us scurrying around, eyeing each other suspiciously?"

"Sort of like stirring an anthill with a stick?" Joe replied. "Could be. The trouble is, sooner or later one of the stunts may go too far. And when that happens, somebody could get hurt."

The yacht sailed from Fort William just after six. By sunset, only the peak of Mount Orange still showed above the horizon. As darkness fell, the sea became rougher. The boat rose and fell like a restless elevator. At the same time, it rolled noticeably from side to side.

The dinner gong sounded while Frank and Joe were on the afterdeck, talking over the day's events. When they stood up to go inside, the unexpected motion of the deck made Frank stumble.

"Oops," he said, grabbing the rail for support. "We're going to need our sea legs tonight."

Joe grinned. "Not to mention strong stomachs," he said. "I wonder who'll show up for dinner."

"After all that pizza, who needs dinner anyway?" Frank replied.

As it turned out, everyone showed up. Sylvie even changed for the occasion. She walked in wearing a navy skirt and gauzy white blouse, with a deep blue scarf loosely knotted at her neck. The gesture earned her a smile of appreciation from Bettina and a carefully composed portrait by Kenneth.

The main course was a delicate, very fresh poached fish in caper sauce, accompanied by tiny new potatoes decorated with sprigs of parsley. Frank thought it was sensationally good and polished his plate. However, whether because of that afternoon's pizzafest or the motion of the boat, most everyone else picked at the food without much interest.

The table was cleared. Arnie carried in the dessert. It was a big glass bowl filled with slices of colorful tropical fruit, topped with scoops of lemon, lime, and orange sorbet. There was a chorus of ooohs and ahs.

"I think I just found more room in my stomach," Boris announced.

"Me, too," Lisa said.

"It looks wonderful," David said. "But I'm going to have to pass."

Several more people said yes to dessert. Arnie had barely finished serving them when Boris clapped a hand over his mouth and jumped to his feet.

"What is it?" Bettina asked in an alarmed voice. "Do you feel ill?"

Boris didn't answer. He ran for the door to the deck.

"I—I don't . . ." Jason started to say. His face

suddenly went pale. He, too, jumped up and ran outside to lean over the rail, Lisa close behind.

Elizabeth sprang to her feet. Her chair clattered to the floor.

"You fools!" she screamed. "Don't you see? We've all been poisoned!"

8 Throwing Up Clues

At Elizabeth's alarmed cry, everyone jumped up from the table.

"Please stay calm," Bettina said, in a voice that cut through the hubbub. "There's no cause for panic."

"Bettina's right," David said. "Some people get seasick more easily, that's all. It's nothing to be nervous about."

"It's poison, I tell you!" Elizabeth wailed, clutching her middle.

Joe was on her left. He took her arm and said in a soothing voice, "Hey, it's okay. Calm down. We'll take care of it."

Elizabeth blinked a few times. She looked at Joe as if she had never seen him before. Then she turned to Bettina. "Please excuse me," she said. "I think I need to rest."

"Do that, dear," Bettina replied.

"You want me to come with you?" Joe asked.

Elizabeth straightened up and returned her nose to its usual airborne position. "Certainly not!" she said. "I am quite in control of myself . . . unlike some people I could name."

She left, taking the door that led upstairs.

"Did you notice something?" Frank murmured to Joe. "For all her talk about poison, she didn't leave in much of a hurry. I don't think she was actually nauseated."

"Daddy?" Evan said, tugging at David's shirt. "I don't feel so good. I think I'm going to be sick."

"Okay, take it easy, son," David said. "You'll be all right. Take deep breaths." He hurried the boy out of the salon. Just then Boris came back in, his face white and drawn.

"Oof!" he said, dropping onto his chair. "Whatever I ate, I hope never to eat it again!"

Arnie was still standing by the buffet, horrified. "Ms. Dunn," he said. "There was nothing wrong with the food, I swear it. All the ingredients were bought fresh this afternoon, from the most reliable sources."

"No one's accusing you or your food," Bettina said.

This diplomatic lie seemed to serve its purpose. Arnie calmed down.

Joe studied the table. It was just as he thought.

"Frank," he said in an undertone. "Everybody who got sick ate dessert. And nobody who skipped dessert got sick."

Frank, too, scanned the table. "You're right," he replied. Aloud, he said, "Arnie? Would you mind if we take a closer look at the fruit compote?"

Arnie's hysteria started to mount again. "There is *nothing* wrong with it!" he declared.

"Then it doesn't matter if we check it out," Joe said. "If we want to waste our time, so what?"

Bettina caught Arnie's eye and nodded. He gave the Hardys an irate look, but he stepped aside.

Joe leaned over the bowl and sniffed deeply. Then he moved back to give Frank room. Frank, too, sniffed the dessert.

"There's something," Frank said.

"Sort of like cough syrup?" Joe replied. "That's what I thought."

Arnie was listening. "This dish is perfectly fine," he said. "I had a portion myself. It was delicious."

"Smell," Joe suggested.

Arnie looked at him suspiciously before lowering his head over the bowl. When he raised it, his expression had changed to one of fury.

"Okay, what clown messed with my *coupe royale des fruits tropicales?*" he shouted, glaring around the table. "Come on, admit it!"

There was an awkward silence. During it, Jason and Lisa came back inside, both pale. Joe hid a smile. Even attacked by nausea, Lisa had kept her miniature tape recorder in her hand.

"Arnie—when did you last taste the fruit cup?" asked Frank.

"Why . . . this afternoon, not long after I made it," the chef told him. "I remember I had just rinsed my bowl when those pizzas arrived."

"And there was nothing wrong with it then?" Frank pursued.

"Nothing!" Arnie declared.

"What then?" Joe asked.

"Then I put it in the galley fridge to chill," Arnie said. "I took it out a little while ago to top it with the sorbets."

"But you didn't try it then?" Cesar asked.

Arnie shook his head. "No. If I had, I would have known something was wrong. I certainly wouldn't have served it. I would have fed it to the fishes."

"I have the feeling anybody can go into the fridge," Frank said. "Right?"

"Sure," Arnie replied. "We keep a shelf loaded with juices, bottled waters, and sodas just for the passengers."

"So if somebody wanted to put something in the fruit, it wouldn't have been hard to do without getting caught," Joe said.

"I guess not," Arnie admitted. "Put that way, we come out sounding pretty careless. Maybe we should change the way we do things. But we're not used to having poisoners as passengers."

"Look, everybody!" Boris shouted from the doorway. "I found it!"

He rushed into the room. In his right hand, held high, was a small brown bottle.

"*What* did you find?" Bettina demanded.

"And where?" Jason added.

Boris handed the bottle to Joe. As soon as Joe saw the label, he understood. "It's ipecacuanha—syrup of ipecac," he said to Frank. "Remember? From that first-aid course?"

Frank snapped his fingers. "I should have guessed!" To the others, he said, "Syrup of ipecac is a powerful emetic. In other words, it makes you throw up. It's used when somebody's swallowed a noncaustic poison and you need to get it out of their system fast."

"You mean somebody put a powerful medication in our food?" Sylvie said. "How could they dare? What if one of us died from it? That would be murder!"

Joe studied the label. "The usual adult dose is a tablespoonful," he reported. "And this whole bottle holds only two tablespoonfuls. Spread across a dozen portions of fruit, there wasn't much chance that anybody would even come close to a normal dose. It must have worked so well because people were already feeling queasy from the rough seas."

"Boris, good job finding this," Frank said. "Where was it?"

Boris beamed. "There is a wastebasket in the rest room next to the galley," he explained. "I found it under some paper towels."

"What made you look there?" Lisa asked.

"I was sure something had been put in the food," Boris replied. "I didn't think the trickster would risk leaving evidence in the galley. But I didn't think whoever it was would want to carry it very far either. So I looked near the galley, and there it was."

"That was very bright," Sylvie burbled.

"And very convenient," Jason said sourly. "It's almost as if you knew where to look."

"What's that supposed to mean?" Boris demanded, clenching his fists, his biceps bulging.

"Oh, nothing," Jason said. "So you spotted it in the wastebasket and you just reached in and picked it up. Didn't you ever hear of fingerprints?"

"Sure I have, wiseguy," Boris retorted. He gave Jason a narrow-eyed stare. "Everybody has. Including whoever put that stuff in the dessert. I figured he must have taken precautions."

"And in case he didn't," Jason pursued, "you made sure that *your* fingerprints were all over the bottle. Not to mention Joe's and Frank's."

Boris gave a low growl and started around the table toward Jason.

Joe quickly blocked his way. "Take it easy," he said. "Don't let him get to you."

"He'd better not let *me* get to *him*," Boris threatened. "When I'm done with him, he'll look like a pretzel!"

Bettina rapped her spoon against the table. "Stop it right now, all of you," she commanded. "I want no more taunts. Joe, Frank—you were starting to ask some very good questions. Please go on."

"Well . . ." Frank said. "There's one obvious question. *Why* did Boris find that bottle?"

Boris let out another growl. Frank held up a hand and said, "No, wait. What I'm getting at is this. There are thousands of square miles of open sea around us. If I wanted to get rid of something, I'd toss it over the side. Poof—gone forever. Why throw it in a wastebasket, where somebody might—where somebody *did*—find it?"

Cesar spoke up. "Simple as A-B-C. Because you want it to be found."

"And for a simple, twisted reason," Sylvie said. Her voice trembled with emotion. "This person wants us to know he is playing tricks on us. He wants us to believe he will play more and worse tricks. He wants to shake us up so we will not do so well in the contest."

For the last twenty minutes, Kenneth had been prowling the room, snapping candid shots of everyone. Now, to Joe's surprise, he spoke. "You're saying it's one of the other contestants?"

For a moment Sylvie looked confused. "I'm not accusing anyone," she insisted. "I don't know who's in back of this. But whoever it is, I think he gets a kick out of seeing us puzzled and upset. And I think that is really nasty!"

"I thoroughly agree, Sylvie," Bettina said. "Ordering those pizzas I can excuse as a juvenile prank. But jeopardizing people's health, even slightly, is another matter. You are all the guests of *Teenway.* If anything happens to you, the good name of *Teenway* is in danger. I won't have that. If these tricks do not stop at once, I shall have to think very seriously about canceling the contest and sending you all home early."

A shocked silence followed this declaration. Bettina looked around the table at each of the teens. Then she walked out of the room.

After that no one was in the mood to socialize. One by one, the contest finalists mumbled good night and drifted away. The Hardys were left with Lisa, Kenneth, and Arnie.

Arnie picked up the big glass bowl. "That compote was primo," he said regretfully. He started toward the door to the galley. "Why couldn't he have put that gunk in something like clam dip instead?"

Arnie left. "Let's go outside," Lisa said. "Maybe there's a moon."

The four went to the aft deck. The sky was lit with stars, but no moon. Joe recalled that he wanted to ask Kenneth about that afternoon. "You came back to the boat early, didn't you?" he said.

"Yes. I hadn't carried enough film into town," Kenneth replied. "I came back for more. Why?"

"You know the phone in the foyer?" Joe continued. "Did you notice anybody using it?"

Kenneth thought. "No. But I was just here for as long as it took to run down to my cabin, grab more film, and split."

Lisa lifted her recorder a little higher as she asked, "Well, Joe and Frank Hardy, do you have a lead as to the identity of the pizza maniac?"

Joe rolled his eyes. "No comment, as usual," he said. "Don't you ever put that thing away?"

"Sure." Lisa grinned. "When I've got my story!"

Joe and Frank kept at Kenneth, but they soon decided he probably didn't know anything relevant. A little later the crew anchored the boat for the night in the lee of a small island. Frank and Joe watched, then went down to their cabin to turn in.

Some time later Joe suddenly woke up. He lay on his bunk in the darkness, listening intently. Something had disturbed him. What?

After a few moments he heard furtive scraping sounds. His mental map told him they were coming from the corridor just outside the door to their cabin. Could it be the burglar returning? Or paying a visit to one of the other cabins?

Stealthily Joe pushed back the covers and stood up. He tiptoed across the dark cabin, felt his way along the wall to the door, and opened it a crack. The light in the corridor, which was left on all the time, was off. A bad sign—someone must have unscrewed a bulb.

A faint, almost indetectable glimmer of light came down the companionway from the main deck. Joe walked silently along the corridor toward it. Suddenly a shape loomed up in front of him, cutting off the light. He sensed, more than saw, two hands reaching out to grab him.

9 In the Bag

The instant he realized that he was under attack, Joe tucked his chin into his chest and dropped into a crouch. Reaching up, he closed both hands around one of his attacker's wrists. Then he did a half spin on the ball of one foot. His opponent's extended arm was now trapped against the fulcrum of his right shoulder. He took a deep breath and prepared to use the power of his thigh muscles to execute a full shoulder throw. Even as he did, he wondered why the other guy was hanging limp instead of resisting.

"Joe, hold on, it's me!" a familiar voice said in his ear. At the same time a hand grabbed the waistband of his pajamas at the back. This was a standard counter to his move. If he went ahead with the throw, he would find himself being pulled along with his opponent.

"Frank? What are you doing here?" Joe asked softly. He released his brother's wrist and straightened up.

"I heard a suspicious noise and got up to check it out," Frank replied, keeping his voice pitched low. "I saw a flickering light up on the main deck, near the head of the stairs. I went to see who it was, but by the time I got there the person had disappeared. What about you?"

"Same as you," Joe said. "But in my case the suspicious noise was you. Did you turn out the hall light?"

"No, it was like that when I came out of our room," Frank said. "I tried the switch. No go. The bulb must be unscrewed."

"So we're not dealing with somebody who just decided to get a midnight snack," Joe remarked.

"No way," Frank told him. "Do you remember where we put the flashlight? I want a closer look at the area near the head of the stairs."

The Hardys found their flashlight and climbed up to the main deck. They searched the foyer and the passage that led to the salon and dining area. They checked the washroom where Boris had found the ipecac bottle. They peered into the galley. Nothing seemed out of place anywhere.

They returned to the head of the companionway.

"Maybe it was just an insomniac after all," Joe said, disgusted.

"An insomniac with a phobia about lightbulbs?" Frank replied. "I don't think so."

"Well, whatever he or she was up to, no traces were left," Joe said. "Let's take another look in the morning."

"I guess you're right," Frank said. He waved the flashlight around for one last look. His voice changed. "Joe—look!"

He had stopped the circle of light on the bulletin board. Crudely painted in black on the white cork surface was a skull and crossbones.

A superstitious thrill touched the back of Joe's neck and ran down his spine. After a moment he recovered his cool. He stepped forward and touched a fingertip to the bulletin board. It felt dry, but when he sniffed his finger there was a faint odor of paint solvent.

"It's pretty fresh," he reported.

"It has to be," Frank replied. "We would have noticed if it had been there when we went to bed."

"A skull and crossbones," Joe mused. "The symbol for poison. And this evening ipecac, stuff that's used in poisoning cases, turned up in the dessert."

Joe paused and stared at the sinister drawing. It seemed to expand to fill his field of vision.

"You know what, Frank?" he continued. "Maybe whoever painted this is the same person who doctored the dessert. I bet this is meant as a threat. It's a warning. The message is, next time they'll use something more harmful than ipecac syrup. Something really poisonous."

"Could be," Frank said. "I can think of another

84

explanation, though. And it's one I like even less than yours."

"What's that?" Joe asked.

Frank cleared his throat. "A couple of hundred years ago this area we're cruising around was infested with bloodthirsty pirates. People like Blackbeard and Captain Kidd, who preyed on innocent sailors and travelers, plundering and killing them. And what was the flag the pirates used? The Skull and Crossbones!"

There was a tense silence. Joe turned his face away from the menacing symbol. As he did, something on the deck caught his eye. It was small and black. He bent down to pick it up. Then he held it out to show to Frank. It was a plastic spider.

"I remember back in grade school," Joe said, "I spent a lot of time drawing a skull and crossbones on the cover of my looseleaf notebook. I must have been about the same age as Evan is now."

"I probably did the same," Frank admitted. "Lots of kids do. But there's a difference between drawing something on your own notebook and painting it on somebody else's wall. Can you really see a kid like Evan sneaking out of his cabin in the middle of the night to spray a pirate symbol on the bulletin board?"

"Well, no, I guess not," Joe said. "And I can't see how he would reach the lightbulbs to unscrew them, either. So maybe Evan dropped a spider here at some other time. Or maybe the prankster deliberately left the spider near the drawing to try to pin the blame on Evan. That would be a really dirty trick."

"Or the prankster could have dropped it by accident," Frank pointed out. "But let's say the same person who painted this put the ipecac in the fruit. Finding this spider here makes it look pretty likely that he stuck the spiders on the cake yesterday, too. And if that's so, it means that once we've solved one puzzle, we'll have solved them all."

Joe held back a yawn. "The sooner the better," he said. "I wouldn't mind having a little time to enjoy the cruise."

Morning came quickly. Just after dawn the boat weighed anchor and started toward its next destination. When the Hardys passed the bulletin board on the way to breakfast, Joe saw that the skull and crossbones had vanished under a fresh coat of white paint. Captain Mathieson obviously ran a tight ship.

After breakfast everyone gathered in the salon. It was time for the second round of the teen-detective contest. David walked to the center of the room. He had a stack of booklets under one arm.

"This morning's trial is a little different," he announced. "For one thing, we haven't attempted to stage it, not even on tape. For another, the focus is on the testimony of witnesses rather than physical evidence. In fact, what I've tried to do is give you something like a classic 'fair play' detective story."

"Oh no," Sylvie groaned. "You mean with timetables? Who did what when? I always skip over those chapters. They just confuse me."

"I don't skip those chapters, I skip the whole book," Jason bragged. "Action, excitement, that's what counts. Not all this intellectual hoo-ha."

Joe saw David's smile flicker.

"I do not agree," Boris said. "The clash of witnesses is exciting. The moment when you see how to prove that someone is lying—that is a thrill."

"I hope you'll find this morning thrilling," David said, cutting short the discussion. "Here is the situation. A famous museum has just held a reception for its most important contributors. Afterward the director discovers that a small but priceless sculpture is missing. She asks you to figure out who took it, without disturbing any innocent contributors or causing a scandal."

Cesar laughed. "I get it. The title of this story is 'Don't Dog the Fat Cats.'"

David ignored Cesar's joke. He held up one of the booklets. "In here you'll find a floor plan of the exhibit and a series of statements by people who were at the reception. You have one hour to read the material, think it over, and decide who the thief is. Guessing won't do the job. You have to say how you identified the guilty party, citing evidence from the booklet. Any questions?"

"Can we use reference materials?" Boris asked.

"All the information you need is in the booklet," David told him. "Anything else? All right. Good luck."

The five finalists took their booklets and fanned out to different parts of the boat. Joe and Frank used this free period to make notes about all the incidents on the voyage so far.

They also found time to talk with Evan. They dropped casual mentions of pirates, poisons, and skulls into the conversation. Evan did not show even a flicker of fear or self-consciousness. Frank looked over at Joe and gave a slight shake of his head. Whoever had defaced the bulletin board, it was clearly not Evan.

Soon the hour was up. While Kenneth took one photograph after another, the contestants handed David their entries. He promised to score them right away and asked them not to discuss their solutions until he had finished.

"Very well," Sylvie said as David went off to his room. "But I have another mystery. Has anyone seen my scarf? I know I wore it last night, and now I do not know where it is. It is blue with green parrots. My favorite uncle brought it back from Paris for me, and I would hate to lose it."

No one had seen it since the night before.

"Hey, Joe," Evan said. "I bet we can find it. Will you look with me?"

"Sure, why not," Joe replied. "Where should we start?"

"How about under the furniture?" Evan suggested. "Whenever I lose something, that's where it always is."

Joe played along. While the others grinned at

"So our trap worked fine, but we didn't catch anything," Frank mused. "Too bad you didn't see who it was."

"I didn't see who it was," Joe replied. "But I can make a very good guess. I recognized the perfume."

The Hardys went looking for Sylvie. They found her sitting in the salon with a magazine open on her lap. She looked up when she heard them approaching. Frank could see her hands tighten on the pages.

"Joe? You are all right?" she asked.

Joe shrugged and didn't reply.

"He'll probably have the mother of all headaches tonight," Frank said. "But I don't think there's any lasting injury."

"That is very good," Sylvie said. She looked down at her magazine as if she thought the exchange was finished . . . or wanted it to be.

"Sylvie," Frank said, "Joe and I need to talk to you. Will you come with us?"

Her face pale, Sylvie followed them onto the deck. Joe dragged three chairs into a tight circle. The moment Sylvie sat down, she covered her face with both hands and started to weep.

Frank glanced around. Jason, Boris, and Cesar were all watching from a distance. When he glared at them, they slowly drifted away.

"I am so sorry," Sylvie sobbed. "I never meant for this to happen. Never!"

"What is your connection with Chuck?" Joe asked.

She dropped her hands to stare at him. "Chuck?"
She dropped her hands to stare at him. "Chuck?"
she said, wiping her cheeks. "I have no connection with Chuck. I do not even know this Chuck."

"You entered our cabin and took that file, didn't you?" Frank demanded.

"But of course I took the file," she replied. "I had to. I am sure Chuck was not working alone. Someone else on the boat is part of his scheme. When you talked about the evidence lying unguarded in your cabin, I was afraid. What if the unknown accomplice took it and destroyed it? We might never reach the truth."

"Hold it right there," Joe said. "Are you trying to tell us you took the file to protect it?"

Sylvie spread out her hands, palms upward. "But of course. To protect it and to use it. You must understand. I *know* I am a good detective. But I did not do so well on the puzzles yesterday or today. Winning the contest is very important to me. It is a chance that will not come again. I thought, if I solve a real mystery, one of importance to the people of *Teenway*, perhaps that will help me in the contest."

"In other words, you stole the file as a way of helping us," Joe said in a tone of disbelief.

"To help you and to help myself," Sylvie replied. "I see now that you set a trap. So you too have understood that the accomplice is still at large."

Joe rolled his eyes and made an incredulous noise. It sounded something like *phfuah!*

"And then, when Joe came after you, you beaned him with a stool and knocked him down a flight of stairs," Frank pointed out. "That's a funny way of helping us."

"I was afraid," Sylvie said with a shrug. "I heard someone chasing me. I thought it was the villain. I had to defend myself. So I hid in the alcove by the telephone and picked up the only weapon I could find. I did not see it was Joe until I was already swinging the stool at him. Then I tried not to hit so hard, but the boat rolled and he fell. I am very sorry. Are you sure you are all right?"

Frank and Joe went on questioning Sylvie for another ten minutes, but she stuck to her story. She had wanted to guard the file of evidence and use it to unmask Chuck's secret accomplice. She had hit Joe in self-defense. She was very, very sorry, but she was also happy Joe had such a thick skull.

"I'd say she took that round on points," Joe muttered, as he and Frank went down to their cabin. "Do you believe her?"

Frank put out his hand, palm down, and wobbled it from side to side. "As Sylvie would say, *comme ci, comme ça.* Or in plain American, six of one, half a dozen of the other."

While Frank made notes about the afternoon's events, Joe took a shower, then sat holding a cold washcloth to his head. Soon it was time for dinner. They reached the main deck just as Arnie stepped out of the galley. He was holding a wooden mallet and a set of chimes.

"Hey, if it isn't the men of the hour," he said. "Time to call everybody to dinner. Would you like to do the honors?"

"Sure," Frank said. He took the chimes and gave Joe the mallet. Joe whanged away, with more enthusiasm than musicality. Finally Arnie reached over and took back the mallet.

The day had been long and full of excitement. It had started with a round of the contest and continued through a picnic on a deserted tropical beach, a near drowning, the unmasking and successful escape of a dirty-tricks artist, a chase, and a dangerous tumble downstairs.

Frank had expected that everyone around the dinner table would be dying to talk about one or another—or all—of these events. Instead, over Cajun-style crawfish stew with dirty rice, they started swapping airport horror stories.

"National is the worst," Elizabeth claimed. "I swear it was built a hundred years ago for the Wright brothers."

"At least you can get there," David said. "Evan and I visited England last summer. We spent nearly as much time going from Manhattan to JFK as from JFK to London!"

Boris grinned. "In America we are lucky," he said. "Where I was born, before the plane takes off, the passengers have to get out and help wind up the rubber bands!"

The table exploded with laughter. When it died down, Sylvie said, "Montreal has a very good modern airport. I like it." She turned to Jason, who was sitting next to her. "What about your home?"

"What, Fort Worth?" Jason shrugged. "The airport's okay, I guess. It's nothing special."

"O'Hare," Kenneth said. "That's the real pits."

"I don't much like O'Hare either," Bettina said. "But landing at St. Hilda the other day was the first time an airport made me think seriously about writing my will."

When everyone finished the main course, Bettina announced that dessert would be served outside on the aft deck. She pretended not to hear when Boris muttered, "That is so we will be closer to the rail, in case there is something in the dessert again tonight."

They went outside. The sea was dark, but overhead the sky was still a pale blue. To the east, night crept up from the horizon. A few early stars glimmered. A cool breeze blew in.

"I think I'll get a sweater," Lisa said with a little shiver. "I'll be right back."

As she left, Arnie appeared carrying a cake with two lit sparklers in it. The frosting was chocolate. On the top, in white frosting, was the outline of a boat and the words *Teenway Detectives*.

"This cake is for everyone who is part of our cruise, but especially in honor of Joe and Frank

Hardy," Bettina announced. "They've shown us what it really means to be teen detectives."

Everyone applauded. Frank looked over at Joe and smiled. It was nice that what they had done so far was appreciated. Now, after a tribute like this, they had no choice but to finish solving the case as quickly as possible.

Arnie cut the cake. Bettina handed the first two pieces to Frank and Joe. Frank was taking his first bite when Lisa ran out onto the deck.

"My tapes!" she cried. "All my tapes are gone! They've been stolen!"

14 A Criminal Record

The rest of the group stared silently at Lisa. Her tapes? All those little cassettes she had so carefully recorded were missing?

Joe could tell that he and Frank were both thinking the same thing. Apparently Lisa had been right when she had suggested that there was important evidence on her tapes. Why else would anyone steal them?

Bettina stepped over to Lisa, put her hands on the girl's shoulders, and said, "How terrible for you. Are you sure? Could you have put them someplace different that slipped your mind?"

"They're gone, I tell you," Lisa repeated. "When I looked in the box where I keep them, all I found was this."

She held up a thick, dog-eared paperback.

"Hey, that's my book," Boris declared. "I left it on deck this morning before the picnic, while I went to get my swimsuit. When I came back, it was gone. I haven't finished it."

"Here," Lisa said. Joe heard an edge of hysteria in her voice. She tossed the book in Boris's direction. "I don't want your dopey book. I want my cassettes back. My whole story about the contest is on them."

She turned to Joe. "You'll find them for me, won't you, Joe?" she pleaded.

"We'll try," Joe promised. "Where was this box?"

"On the table in my cabin," Lisa replied. "I can't believe I was such a dodo, leaving it out like that. The first day I kept the box in the drawer under my bed. But it was too much of a hassle to get it out every time I wanted to put away another tape or listen to an earlier one."

"Was your cabin locked?" Frank asked.

Lisa's cheeks turned pink. "No. I . . . I have a thing about losing keys. I'm always getting locked out of places because I lose my key. So I don't lock up if I can help it. I know that sounds dumb."

"I guess I don't have to ask if the box was locked," Joe said. He gave Lisa a reassuring smile. "What does it look like?"

A confused expression crossed Lisa's face. "The box?" she said. "But it's not gone. Oh—you mean what is it like? It's a nice old wooden box with an

128

attached lid. I guess it was meant as a jewelry box. It's just the right size for my recorder and a bunch of cassettes."

"Do you keep your recorder in there, too?" Joe asked.

"When I'm not using it, sure," Lisa replied. "Of course, I had it with me today."

"Of course," Elizabeth echoed in a snide tone.

"I can see why somebody might steal your tape recorder," Kenneth said. "That's an expensive piece of equipment. But why would anyone want a lot of used cassettes?"

"It's not the cassettes, Kenneth, it's what's on them," Cesar told him. "Look at the way Lisa's been snooping around ever since this trip began. Almost anybody might want to get rid of them."

Lisa's eyes blazed. "The only people who have something to fear are people who have something to hide," she retorted. "How about you, Cesar? What are *you* trying to hide?"

"My urge to pour a glass of lemonade over your head," Cesar promptly replied.

"This isn't getting us anywhere," Joe pointed out. "Lisa, when was the last time you saw the missing tapes?"

"I put a couple of cassettes in the box when we came back from the beach," Lisa replied. "Everything was okay then."

"Call it four o'clock," Frank mused. "And you realized just now the cassettes were missing. So that's about a five-hour stretch when the theft could have happened. Were you in your cabin for any part of that time?"

"I took a nap," Lisa said. She sounded embarrassed, as if naps were only for little kids and old people. "From about four-thirty to five-thirty. Then I came out on deck. I got here a little while before you and Joe tangled with that guy."

"This is a waste of time," Cesar said. "Her room was wide open and the box was in plain sight. How long would it take somebody to duck inside, grab the cassettes, and split? She might as well have left them in the salon with a little sign that said Free— Take One."

"You sound as if you know all about it," Elizabeth remarked. "I wonder why."

"Listen, you—" Cesar growled.

"Don't you call me 'you,'" Elizabeth snapped.

"What am I supposed to call you? 'Him'?" Cesar retorted.

"That's quite enough," Bettina declared. "We're all overexcited and overtired. We're starting to say things we don't mean, things we'll regret in the morning. Let's enjoy this wonderful cake our chef has made for us. If Joe and Frank have questions to ask about Lisa's tapes, they can do it one on one."

Frank awoke very early the next morning. A faint gray light shone through the porthole over his bed. A slight vibration and a difference in the motion of the boat told him that they were under way again.

He sat up, slipped on shorts, a tank top, and a pair of boat mocs, and tiptoed out of the cabin without waking Joe.

Two levels up, he went out onto the walkway past the pilot house. Captain Mathieson, at the helm, waved and called, "Good morning." At the front of the pilot house, a companionway led down to the bow. This was a working area of the yacht, not meant for passengers. Instead of comfortable seats and teak coffee tables, there were two big coils of inch-thick rope and a grease-specked power winch used for hoisting the anchor.

Frank rested his arms on the metal rail. By leaning out, he could watch the wave of white foam cast up by the boat's bow. The individual lines of bubbles constantly changed form, but the general shape of the wave remained the same. Like this case. The details changed, but the basic questions remained the same. Who was Chuck's accomplice? What was on Lisa's cassettes that was so dangerous to the conspiracy?

A tiny island appeared off to starboard. A patch of grass no bigger than a tennis court, with a single wind-twisted tree ringed by a beach of white sand. Just beyond it, a thirty-foot sailboat swung at anchor. A man in the cockpit noticed Frank and waved. Frank waved back. Then he returned to his thoughts.

The investigation the night before had been a bust. Everyone had been down to the cabin deck at some point before dinner. Anyone could have slipped in and taken Lisa's cassettes. No one had seen anything suspicious. Finally, before turning in for the night, Frank and Joe had taken David and Bettina aside to propose a daring plan. The participants in the contest were all supposed to be talented teen detectives. Why not put them to work detecting?

After half an hour Frank went to the galley and cadged a mug of hot coffee and a freshly baked cinnamon roll from Arnie.

"I've been thinking," Arnie told him as he sliced bacon for breakfast. "About Chuck. He's not the guy who invented the wheel, if you get my drift. He must have had somebody else telling him what to do."

"You think so?" Frank replied, his tone casual. "Any idea who?"

Arnie paused with his knife in the air. "Not specifically," he said. "But I'd bet it was a guy. Chuck is a little backward in his thinking. He would have a problem taking orders from a girl."

"Did you notice him talking to any of the passengers?" Frank asked.

Arnie shook his head. "Nope. Sorry." He grinned. "We're not supposed to fraternize. Company policy."

Frank grinned back. "Is that what we're doing? Fraternizing? And I thought I was just stealing one of these awesome cinnamon buns . . . or two!"

Frank refilled his mug and went back to the bow.

An island was just peeping above the horizon, dead ahead. For the next twenty minutes or so, as it grew larger, he leaned on the rail and let his mind wander. Then he went in to make sure Joe was up and getting ready for breakfast.

After breakfast everyone gathered in the salon. David seemed ill at ease as he said, "We have decided to do something a little different for today's round in the teen-detective contest. In a minute I'll pass out a booklet with summaries of all the incidents that have marred our cruise these last few days."

"You mean that's the mystery we have to solve?" Elizabeth asked.

David nodded. "Right. Your assignment is to decide what Chuck's role was and whether he was working alone. If not, who was his accomplice? You should back up your opinions with reasoning and evidence."

Cesar raised his hand. "Are we limited to using the evidence in the booklet?"

David glanced quickly at Frank, who shook his head.

"No, you're not," David told Cesar. "Any information you have, you can use. But if it's not in the booklet, you have to explain how you know it. We'll reconvene in one hour."

Before the hour was up, the yacht arrived at its next port of call, Galleon Bay on the island of St. Mark. The town was built on three sides of the wide bay, which was thick with sailboats and motor cruisers. The *Colombe d'Or,* the biggest craft in port, was given a place of honor alongside a waterfront boulevard called the Embarcadero.

When the time expired, everyone reassembled in the salon. David collected the five entries. Then he said, "At this point I'm going to turn the chair over to the Hardys. Joe, Frank?"

"Who wants to go first?" Joe asked, looking around the circle.

After an awkward silence Boris said, "I will. Chuck did not have an accomplice. The odds are against finding two conspirators in such a small group."

"Pure guesswork." Elizabeth sniffed. "How could one person have done everything?"

"He didn't," Boris replied. "But he did not have an accomplice. Someone else was playing little jokes on his own . . . just as he did on the flight down, with his spiders. It was Evan who painted the skull and crossbones and hid Sylvie's scarf under the couch where he later found it."

David pressed his lips together. Joe could see that he was furious about this attack on his son.

"Aw, come on," Cesar protested. "Are you saying Evan bought the syrup of ipecac, too? He wasn't even ashore!"

"Hold it," Frank said. "Let's hear what everyone has to say before we start arguing. Who's next? Sylvie?"

Sylvie twisted her fingers together and stared at

the floor. "I think Chuck was working with one of us to wreck the contest," she said in a low voice. "Most of us want very much to win and want very much for the contest to be a success. We would not wreck it. But there is one who seems to care nothing about the contest. I do not know why she would want to wreck it, but that is the only answer I can see."

Everyone turned to look at Elizabeth. Her face turned red. "Ridiculous!" she exclaimed. "Totally lame!"

"What is your solution?" Joe asked her.

"Chuck was working alone," Elizabeth replied.

"What about the times on the drugstore receipt and the pizza order?" Boris demanded. "How could he be in two places at once?"

"He wasn't," Elizabeth said. "The cash register at the pharmacy had the time wrong, that's all."

Boris gave a sarcastic laugh and said, "Talk about lame!"

Frank turned to Cesar. "What about you?" he asked.

Cesar was visibly troubled. "I don't think I want to say anything," he announced. "Solving mystery puzzles is fun. This is different. This involves real people. What if somebody accuses me? I will be very hurt, even though I know I am innocent. So how can I do this to someone else? I wrote down what I had to say. When David reads it, he can decide if it makes any sense."

There was a short silence. Then Jason said, "That

leaves me. Yeah, there's a conspiracy, all right. But Chuck has nothing to do with it."

Everybody started talking at once. Jason held up his hand. "Yo, let me say my piece! Okay, so Chuck ran away. What does that prove? Nada! You might do the same—if you figured out you were being framed by a couple of hotshot detectives."

"Oh, now, wait a minute," Lisa said. "Are you trying to tell us—"

"You got it, sister," Jason said. "All those stunts were pulled by none other than Frank and Joe Hardy! They set up the whole thing so they could solve it and get their faces on the cover of *Teenway*. We have all been had!"

"Any reaction to that?" David asked Frank.

"Sure," Frank said. "The best defense is a good offense."

"What is that supposed to mean?" Jason demanded.

"If Chuck had an accomplice among our group, it means that one of us is not who he or she seems to be," Frank said.

Joe picked up the thread. "We couldn't figure out who that might be . . . until the imposter blew his cover. Jason—last night you said the airport in your hometown is pretty ordinary."

"Yeah, so?" Jason replied. "It's an airport."

"In fact," Frank said, "the airport that serves Fort Worth is one of the two or three largest and most modern in the world. It's bigger than the whole island of Manhattan. Fort Worth shares it with Dallas. How is it you didn't know that?''

"Big deal," Jason sneered. "Did you ever look at a map of Texas? Dallas and Fort Worth are practically the same town."

"Now I know you're an imposter," Joe said. "Anyone who's really from Fort Worth would eat his boots and ten-gallon hat before saying his town has *anything* in common with Dallas . . . except that enormous airport you didn't seem to know about."

"Another thing," Frank said. "When we were in Fort William, you seemed to find your way awfully easily. Have you spent time around here before?"

"This is a load of garbage," Jason declared. "Why would I want to wreck the *Teenway* contest?"

"Maybe it has something to do with this," Frank said. He held up Jason's portable CD player. Unsnapping the flap of the leather case, he continued, "There's a name written on the inside. Your name. Your *full* name—Jason Mares MacFarlane."

15 Race to the Finish

"Give me that!" Jason shouted. He rushed Frank and grabbed the CD player. "You can't mess with my property!"

Bettina stared at him, openmouthed. "You're Walter's grandson," she said. "I thought you looked familiar. You're a lot like him. Didn't you spend a day at the office with him a couple of years ago?"

"That's right," Jason said, venom dripping from his voice. "That was just before you and your buddies stole his magazine and broke his heart."

"I can understand how it would seem that way to you," Bettina said in a steady voice. "There were a lot of considerations involved that the general public didn't know about."

Jason turned his back on her. To Frank and Joe he said, "Okay, gumshoes. What now? Are you going

138

to have me arrested? For what—a couple of harmless practical jokes? That'll look great when it hits the papers."

Frank looked over at Joe. They both remembered the reasons David and Bettina had given for letting Chuck go. All their arguments applied even more strongly to Jason.

"What about my tapes?" Lisa demanded. "What did you do with them?"

"Get out of my face," Jason told her. "I wouldn't touch your tapes with a barge pole. There's nothing on them I care about anyway."

"Let's just clear up a few things," Joe said. "Were you the one who put David's computer on the outbound luggage cart the day we arrived?"

Jason laughed. "Sure! It nearly worked, too."

"And after the first puzzle, you broke into our cabin, didn't you?" Frank said. "What were you after?"

"Nothing in particular," Jason replied. "I figured it would raise questions about the results."

"And you sent me that terrible article about the boat?" Sylvie asked. "Why me?"

"No reason," Jason told her. "I jabbed my finger at the list of finalists and hit your name."

"And the spiders on the cake?" Frank asked. "I can't see how you did that."

"Simple—I didn't." Jason smirked. "On the plane I held on to some of Evan's spiders, just in case I found a use for them. Then I passed them to Chuck. He's the one who put them on the cake."

"And then he accidentally dropped one while he was painting that skull and crossbones," Joe said. "And the ipecac—you bought it, he put it in the fruit. Then one of you shoved the paper bag, the receipt, and Sylvie's scarf under the sofa for us to find."

"That was *not* nice!" Sylvie hissed.

Jason spread his hands. "Hey, nothing personal. I saw the scarf lying there and I used it, that's all. I didn't even know whether it was yours or Miss Snobbo's. Besides, that turned out to be a major goof. The receipt tipped off our heroes here that Chuck was working with somebody else. If they hadn't found it, they'd never have figured it out."

"Don't be so sure," Frank said. "By the way, how did you swing getting chosen as a finalist in the contest? Did you have help from somebody on the *Teenway* staff who still feels loyal to your grandfather?"

"That's enough," Jason said coldly. "Here's the program. I'm going to go get my pack and I'm going to walk off this tub without anybody hassling me. I'll make it back to St. Hilda on my own. Got it?"

Frank glanced at Bettina, then at David. Both nodded grimly.

"Got it," Frank said. Then, on his own, he added, "But you might not get the welcome you're expecting. We're going to call your grandfather and tell him exactly what you've been up to."

"Yeah," Joe said. "You think he'll jump for joy when he finds out you've been trying to wreck the magazine he founded and spent years making into a success? You think he'll like it when he finds out his grandson is a little sneak?"

"Shut up!" Jason twisted at the waist and cocked his right fist, ready to punch Joe in the face. Joe waited calmly. He wasn't about to pick a fight with Jason, but he certainly wasn't going to back away from one, either.

Boris stepped forward and grabbed Jason's wrist. Jason tried to pull loose, but Boris was much stronger than he.

"If you're going, you had better go now," Boris said in his ear. "If you stay, we may prove to you how unpopular you have just become."

"I'm going," Jason muttered. Boris released him, and he walked off toward the stairs without another word. What he had meant to make a triumphant escape had turned into a crushing retreat.

Elizabeth turned to Sylvie. "I can't believe you thought I was the one!" she declared.

"I'm sorry," Sylvie said. "It's just—"

"Don't be sorry," Elizabeth said, cutting her off. "It's rather . . . exciting. I never saw myself as the adventurous sort. Maybe I should try it."

Boris went over to David. "Where is Evan?" he asked. "I want to apologize."

"The chef is giving him a fishing lesson," David replied. "Since he didn't hear you accuse him, there's no need to apologize. Forget it."

"I will try," Boris said. "It will not be easy. I do not like seeing myself be made a fool."

Lisa came running in. Frank had not noticed her leaving. "Hey, everybody," she shouted. "I've got it!"

"You found the cassettes?" Kenneth asked. "Where were they?"

"No, I didn't find them," Lisa told him. "But I figured it out. If Jason didn't take them, it must have been Chuck. But he didn't have them with him when he jumped off the boat. So they must still be here somewhere. He must have hidden them."

"Okay," Boris said. "The boat is only a hundred and sixty feet long and twenty-five feet wide, with four or five levels. If we start searching now . . ."

"Cut it out. I *know* where to look," Lisa said. "Once I figured out he'd taken them, I asked one of the other crew members a few questions. Guess what? After Chuck brought us back from the picnic, he volunteered to reorganize the supply closet in the galley. He must have hidden my cassettes there!"

Everybody trooped into the galley. It was a tight fit. There was only enough room for one person in the supply closet. The others delegated Frank to do the search. The closet had shelves from floor to ceiling. Each shelf had an elastic cord across the front to keep things from sliding off in rough seas.

Frank started at the bottom left and worked his way up and around. The third shelf held half a dozen boxes of fancy English crackers to serve with cheese. When he tilted one box forward, he saw a plastic freezer bag behind it. The bag was filled with tiny cassettes. They were not dated, but each one was numbered. Before announcing his discovery, Frank pawed through the bag, took out the cassette with the highest number, and hid it in his pocket.

Lisa was overjoyed. "I told you we'd find them here!" she crowed. "You see, Joe? You're not the only detective on this boat!"

"Far from it," Joe said with a glance at the four remaining contest finalists.

Frank took David aside. "Am I right that you brought a microcassette recorder with you? May I borrow it for a few minutes?"

"Sure, it's in my cabin," David replied. "I'll go get it. Do you want to come along?"

Frank got the recorder, then collected Joe. They went to the top-level sundeck. As usual, it was deserted. Frank put the cassette in the recorder. "Assuming Lisa numbered them in order," he explained, "this should be the most recent."

He pressed the Play button. The person speaking was in the middle of a sentence.

". . . *Chuck talking to on the phone?*"

"That's Cesar's voice," Joe said.

"Shhh!" Frank hissed.

"*Good question,*" Joe's voice answered. "*Offhand, I'd guess some friend who was in on his plans. . . .*"

Frank pressed the Stop button.

"You see what this means, don't you?" he asked.

Joe nodded. "I sure do."

Two decks below, the lunch chimes sounded.

143

The Hardys were the last to come to the table. As they sat down, Evan was asking, "Are we going to be here long?"

"Why?" David replied.

"We could go horseback riding," Evan said. "Arnie says the trails are totally awesome. You can swim under a waterfall."

"With your horse?" Boris asked.

"No, silly." Evan laughed. "You get off the horse to go swimming. Can we, Daddy? It's really fun here, but there's not many places to go when you're on a boat."

"We'll see," David said.

There was a short silence while bowls of mussel salad and cracked crab legs were placed on the table. As people began to serve themselves, Frank said, "Lisa? When I found your cassettes, I took one of them out of the bag."

He handed it to her. She glanced at the label. Her face went white. "Did you listen to this?" she asked breathlessly.

Frank nodded. "Is there anything you want to tell us?" he asked.

Lisa coughed twice, then said, "Uh . . . Listen, people—I have to say something. Something important."

Everyone stopped talking to listen.

"The thing is . . ." She stopped to swallow. "Nobody stole my cassettes. I made it up. Then I hid them and pretended to find them."

In the silence that followed, Bettina asked, "Why, Lisa?"

"I wanted to write about it in my article," Lisa told her. "I figured if I was the victim of a crime and I solved it myself, my article would be so hot that you'd have to run it in *Teenway.* I'd be on my way to becoming a rich and famous writer, just as I've always dreamed."

"Not many writers become rich and famous, Lisa," Bettina said. "But if what they write is true and honest, they have other satisfactions. If they write lies, they have to live with those. And sooner or later their lies catch up with them."

"I'm sorry I tried to fool everybody," Lisa said. Her eyes glistened. "I'm still going to write an article about the cruise. But in it I'm going to explain how I was tempted to do something dishonest. And I'm going to explain how my plan was foiled by two brilliant detectives, Joe and Frank Hardy."

"Hey," Boris called. "How did you foil her plan anyway?"

"We listened to the last cassette in the series," Frank said. "It was from yesterday afternoon, when all of us were talking about Chuck's escape. But how could he have stolen a tape of a conversation that happened after he'd jumped ship?"

Boris laughed. "Brilliant! And simple, like many brilliant ideas."

"Speaking of brilliant," David said, "I have an

important announcement. As you all know, the *Teenway* teen detective contest is scheduled to continue through two more puzzles. Given everything that's happened—"

"Oh, you're not cancelling it!" Sylvie wailed. "You can't, not now!"

"We're not," David assured her. "However, having only four finalists still in the contest does make a difference."

"I know—you're going to cut back on the number of prizes," Boris said gloomily.

"Not at all," Bettina assured him. "I just got off a call with my publisher, giving some advance warning of today's startling developments. We discussed what to do about the prize situation. Our decision was to add a special grand prize to the three awards already offered."

The four teen finalists looked at one another. It seemed to Frank that they found it hard to believe what they were hearing.

"In other words," David added, "you are all sure to win an award."

"*Yes-s-ss!*" Boris shouted, and turned to give Cesar a high-five. Elizabeth grabbed Sylvie and gave her a big hug. Sylvie was so surprised by Elizabeth's gesture that she started talking rapidly in French. Kenneth was taking so many pictures that his camera almost smoked.

"By the way, who's ahead?" Boris wondered, when the excitement died down.

"The first puzzle, the body in the captain's

office, was pretty much a wash," Frank reported. "No outstandingly good—or bad—performances."

"And no one spotted the wallet being handed off in the second puzzle," Joe added. "However, Cesar finished that one ahead on points. He remembered the most details. Sylvie was second."

"And as you know," David said, "Cesar's solution to the museum caper was clearly the most on target."

"I start to detect a pattern," Boris said. Frank did not think he sounded displeased.

"But what about real life?" Sylvie said. "This morning, all of us told our solutions to the dirty tricks, and all of us were wrong. But Cesar never said what he had written."

"True," David said. "Cesar, what did you write about this morning's problem?"

Cesar shrugged. "Albuquerque is not that far from Fort Worth," he said. "To fly to New York, I had to change planes at Dallas–Fort Worth. So I knew when Jason made that remark about the airport that he was not who he pretended to be. From that, I assumed that he might be Chuck's accomplice, who could not have done everything. But unlike Frank and Joe, I did not take the next steps and figure out who he really is and why he did what he did."

"Perhaps not, but you did a magnificent job," Bettina declared. "And you already had a substantial lead in the scores. I'm not going to prejudge the contest—"

"No, no, please don't!" David exclaimed. "Frank and Joe and I still have a couple of great puzzles to spring on everyone."

"So I won't say any more," Bettina concluded. "Except to wish all of the contestants continued good luck."

Cesar slapped Frank and Joe on the shoulder. "With these guys on the case," he said, "solving mysteries is never a matter of luck!"

Do your younger brothers and sisters want to read books like yours?

Let them know there are books just for *them!*

They can join Nancy Drew and her best friends as they collect clues and solve mysteries in

THE NANCY DREW NOTEBOOKS®

Starting with

#1 The Slumber Party Secret

#2 The Lost Locket

#3 The Secret Santa

#4 Bad Day for Ballet

AND

Meet up with suspense and mystery in Frank and Joe Hardy: The Clues Brothers™

Starting with

#1 The Gross Ghost Mystery

#2 The Karate Clue

#3 First Day, Worst Day

#4 Jump Shot Detectives

Look for a brand-new story every other month at your local bookseller

A MINSTREL® BOOK

Published by Pocket Books   1366-02

Do your younger brothers and sisters want to read books like yours?

Let them know there are books just for them!

THE NANCY DREW NOTEBOOKS ®

Look for a brand-new story every other month

Available from Minstrel® Books
Published by Pocket Books

1356-02